PAPA BOUCHARD

She had asked him to button her glove.

PAPA BOUCHARD

BY

MOLLY ELLIOT SEAWELL

Illustrated by

WILLIAM GLACKENS

NEW YORK
CHARLES SCRIBNER'S SONS
1901

University Press
JOHN WILSON AND SON, CAMBRIDGE, U. S. A

Illustrations

Illustrations

viii

Illustrations

Illustrations

x

Illustrations

xi

Papa Bouchard

Chapter I

ON a certain day in June, 1901, a cataclysm occurred in the quiet apartment of Mademoiselle Celeste Bouchard, in the Rue Clarisse, the quietest street in the quietest part of Paris. This catacylsm consisted of the simultaneous departure, or rather the levanting, of the entire masculine element in the excellent old lady's household. And this masculine element had been so admirably trained! Monsieur Paul Bouchard, in particular, ten years his sister's junior, was reckoned a model man. Mademoiselle could truly say that during Monsieur Bouchard's fifty-four years of life he had never, until then, given her a moment's anxiety. All the elderly ladies of the

Papa Bouchard

Bouchards' acquaintance pointed with admiration to Monsieur Paul.

"Look!" they said; "such a good brother! Mademoiselle boasts that although he is fifty-four years of age he is still as obedient to her as he was at fifteen. So prosperous and respected as an advocate, too!" And all these ladies sighed because they had not succeeded in petticoating a brother or a husband as Mademoiselle Bouchard had petticoated the prosperous and respected Monsieur Paul Bouchard.

Pierre, the husband of Élise, Mademoiselle Bouchard's maid for thirty years, was as well disciplined as his master, for he was Monsieur Paul's valet. He had never had a will of his own since the day, thirty years before, when Élise had sworn before the altar to love, honor and obey him.

The third masculine creature in the dovecote of the Rue Clarisse was the parrot, Pierrot. Nobody knew exactly how old Pierrot was, but he was sup-

2

posed to have arrived at years of discretion. Mademoiselle had spent a dozen patient years in curing Pierrot of a propensity to bad language, and she had taught him a great variety of moral maxims that made him a model bird, as Monsieur Bouchard was a model man and Pierre a model servant. It is true that Léontine de Meneval, Monsieur Paul's ward, married to a handsome scapegrace captain of artillery, had amused herself with teaching the bird a number of phrases, such as " Bad boy Bouchard " and others reflecting on " Papa Bouchard," as she called him. And Pierrot had picked up these naughty expressions with astonishing quickness. But Léontine had always been regarded as incorrigible by her guardian and his sister, although they really loved her, and since her marriage she had become gayer, merrier and more irresponsible than ever. This deterioration both Monsieur and Mademoiselle Bouchard laid at the door of her husband, Captain de Meneval, with his laughing eyes and devil-may-care manner; with whom, however, aside from these characteristics, not the slightest fault could be found. He was devoted to Léontine, and if the two chose to lead a life as merry and unreflecting as that of the birds in the shadowy forests, nobody could stop them. Papa Bouchard — as the artillery captain had the impudence to call him — did, it is true, keep a tight hand on Léontine's fortune, and would allow her only half her income, at which Léontine grumbled and incited Captain de Meneval to grumble, too. But Papa Bouchard, having full power as trustee, met their complaints and protests with a proposition to cut down their allowance to one-fourth of their income, at which the two young people grew frightened, and desisted.

Now, there dwells in every masculine breast a germ of lawlessness that no discipline ever invented can wholly kill.

Papa Bouchard

Man or parrot, it is the same. After having been brought up in the way he should go, he longs to go it. Such was the case with Pierrot, with Pierre and with Monsieur Bouchard.

It was the bird that first made a dash for liberty.

After ten years of irreproachable conduct, Pierrot, on that June morning, suddenly jumped from the balcony, where he had been walking the railing in the most sedate manner, and scuttled off in the direction of the Alcazar d'Été, the Ambassadeurs, the Moulin Rouge, and the very gayest quarter of Paris.

Monsieur Bouchard was sitting on the balcony at the time. He was rather younger looking, with his clean-shaven face and wiry figure, than most men of his age, but thanks to Mademoiselle Celeste, he patronized the same tailors that had made for his father and his grandfather. Their cut and style indicated that they had been tailors to Cardinal Richelieu and others of that time, and they dressed Monsieur Bouchard in coats and trousers and waistcoats of the pliocene age of tailoring. As for his hats, they might have been dug out of Pompeii, for any modernity they had, and the result was that Monsieur Bouchard's back and legs looked about seventy-five, while his face looked little more than forty.

Instead of giving the alarm when Pierrot trotted gaily off, Monsieur

6

Papa Bouchard

Bouchard felt a strange thrill of sympathy with the runaway.

"Poor devil!" thought he. "No doubt he is sick of the Rue Clarisse — tired of the moral maxims — weary of the whole business. He is n't so young as he was, but there's a good deal of life in him still" — Pierrot was just scampering around the corner — "and he wants to see life."

"There is a psychologic moment for everything," so Otto von Bismarck said. The parrot's escape made a psychologic moment for Monsieur Bouchard, and quietly putting on his hat, and telling Mademoiselle Bouchard that he was going to a meeting of the Society of French Antiquarians at St. Germains, and afterward for a stroll through the museum in the town, made straight for a street in the neighborhood of the Champs

Papa Bouchard

Élysées. He remembered seeing in that quarter a handsome new apartment house lately finished and thoroughly modern. He had for curiosity's sake entered it. He had seen furnished apartments so bright, so light, so cheery, so merry that he longed to establish himself there. He had gone back once, twice, thrice, each time more infatuated with the place. Today he walked in, selected a vacant apartment, and in ten minutes had taken a lease of it for a year.

And then he had to go back to the Rue Clarisse to tell about it.

Of course, he had not thrown off the yoke of thirty years without secret alarms, agitations and palpitations. He walked up and down the Rue Clarisse twice, his heart thumping loudly against his ribs, before he could screw up resolution to enter. He was nerved, however, by the recollection of the apartment he had just seen; it had been given up the day before by a young journalist,

Papa Bouchard

named Marsac, who had left various
souvenirs of a very pleasant life there.
The street was such a bustling, noisy
street — and the Rue Clarisse was so
quiet, so quiet! In the new street there
were two music halls in full view and
generally in full blast, gay restaurants
blazing with lights, where all sorts of
delicious, indigestible things to eat were
to be had, and such an atmosphere of
jollity and movement! Monsieur Bouchard quivered with delight like a schoolboy as he thought of it, and so he marched
in to take his life in his hand while
breaking the news to his sister Celeste.

Mademoiselle Bouchard, a small,
prim, devoted, affectionate, obstinate
creature, was sitting in the drawing-
room, bemoaning with Élise the loss of
Pierrot. Élise, a hard-featured, hard-
working creature, had such a profound
contempt for the other sex that it was
a wonder she ever brought herself to
marry one of them. She was saying to
Mademoiselle Bouchard:

Papa Bouchard

"Depend on it, Mademoiselle, that ungrateful Pierrot will never come back of his own accord. If he had been a she bird, now — but Pierrot is like the rest of his sex. It's in them to run away — and run away they will."

"He has had a quiet, peaceful home in the Rue Clarisse for seventeen years," wailed poor Mademoiselle Bouchard.

"That's reason enough for him to run away. What does he care about a quiet, peaceful home? He wants to be strutting around in some restaurant, drinking and swearing and turning night into day. They're all like that. My Pierre, now, is just as ready to run away as was Pierrot, but I shall keep an eye on *him*."

And then Monsieur Bouchard walked in, with an affectation of ease and debonairness, and told about the apartment near the Champs Élysées, whereat it seemed to poor Mademoiselle Celeste as if the Louvre had moved itself over into the Bois de Boulogne and the Seine

With an affectation of ease and debonairness, and told about the apartment near the Champs Élysées.

had suddenly begun to flow backward. Of course, Monsieur Bouchard had arranged a plausible tale by which his hegira was to appear the most natural and laudable thing in the world. Most men are inventive enough in the matter of personal justification. But it is one thing to make up and tell a plausible tale, and another to get that tale believed. Élise openly sniffed at the theory advanced by Monsieur Bouchard that it was absolutely necessary for him to live nearer the courts. Also, that he was really inspired by a desire to save Mademoiselle the annoyance of clients coming and going.

"You remember, my dear Celeste, you complained of Captain de Meneval the last time he was here. You said he talked and laughed so much, and chucked Élise under the chin ——"

"But that was a trifle; you know there's no real harm done," protested Mademoiselle Bouchard.

"Why? Because I won't let him,"

Papa Bouchard

said Monsieur Bouchard, with the determined air a man assumes when he
wishes to impress a woman with a
great notion of the power he holds
over another man. "It is because he
has to deal with *me* — a man born
with his shirt on, as the peasants say.
Otherwise, there might be harm done.
De Meneval is very saucy. When I
reminded him the other day of the
promise I exacted from him when he
married Léontine, that he would n't
go into debt, the fellow grinned and
said he was in love with Léontine,
and would have promised to eat his
grandmother if I had made that a
condition."

"But in reference to this strange
notion of yours about taking an apartment at your time of life ——"

"That's just it, my dear," cried
Monsieur Bouchard. "I am too old
not to have a separate establishment."

"Too old!" cried Mademoiselle,
who had never ceased to regard the

model Monsieur Bouchard as a wild
sprig of flamboyant youth ; " you mean
too young ! "

Monsieur Bouchard was tickled.
What gentleman of fifty-four is not
pleased at the assumption that he is
merely a colt, after all ?

Mademoiselle Bouchard anxiously
scrutinized her brother. There was a
lawless gleam in his eye — an indefin-
able something that is revealed when a
man has the bit between his teeth and
does not mean to let it go. Mademoiselle, good, innocent soul, was not devoid
of sense, and she saw her only game
was to play for time.

" Very well, Paul. If you *will* desert the Rue Clarisse, I will look about
and get you an apartment near by, and
I will let you have Pierre ———"

" Oh, no, no ! " cried Monsieur Bouchard, hastily. He had no mind to
have a domestic Vidocq in his new
quarters. " I could n't think of rob-
bing you of Pierre. Thirty years you

have had him. You could not get on without him."

" Yes, I could."

" I can't accept the sacrifice."

" I make it cheerfully for your sake."

" It would be cruel to Pierre."

" *He* will make the sacrifice."

" That he will," interrupted Élise, with the freedom of an old servant. " He will caper at the notion of leaving the Rue Clarisse for some wild, dissipated place such as Monsieur Paul has selected."

" Monsieur Paul has not selected a place, Élise," replied Mademoiselle, with severity.

" But — but I have, my dear Celeste. It is No. 25 Rue Bassano. I have taken it for a year. In fact, the van is coming to-day for my personal belongings. Pierre will see to them. And, my dear, I have a busy day before me. I am due at the meeting of the Society of French Antiquarians at St. Germains at one o'clock, and I can

barely make the train. Afterward I
shall spend some instructive hours in
the museum — I shall see you to-morrow — " and Monsieur Bouchard literally ran out of the room.

" There he goes ! " apostrophized
Élise to Mademoiselle Celeste, who
was almost in tears. " That's the
way Pierrot scampered off, and Pierre
wants only half a wink to run off, too,
to the Rue Bassano."

" Élise," cried Mademoiselle, " you
are most unjust, and your suspicions of
Pierre will be disproved. Ring the
bell."

Pierre appeared.

He was about Monsieur Bouchard's
age, height and size — medium in
all respects — clean shaven, like his
master, and wore a cast-off suit of
Monsieur Bouchard's, as it was the
morning and his livery was religiously
saved for the afternoon. He was, in
short, a very good replica of Monsieur
Bouchard.

Papa Bouchard

Mademoiselle Bouchard stated the case to him, carefully giving Monsieur Paul's bogus reasons.

" The Rue Bassano is a very gay and noisy place, Pierre, as you know, with a great many theatres and restaurants about, and much passing to and fro. It will be a change from the Rue Clarisse."

" Mademoiselle, I know it," Pierre replied, showing the whites of his eyes. " I would much rather remain in this decent, quiet street."

Mademoiselle turned to Élise with an I-told-you-so air, and said, " No doubt you would, Pierre — a man of your excellent character."

" Yes, Mademoiselle. The theatres and music halls must be very objectionable — and the restaurants. I suppose the waiters would laugh at me when I went to fetch Monsieur's dinner of boiled mutton and rice."

" Yes ; but if it were your duty to go with Monsieur ? "

Papa Bouchard

" Duty, Mademoiselle, has ever been a sacred word with me. Though but a servant, I have always revered my duty," replied the virtuous Pierre. He backed and filled for some time longer, as servants commonly do — and as some of their masters and mistresses do sometimes — but finally, in response to Mademoiselle Bouchard's pleading that he would not desert Monsieur Bouchard at this critical moment in his career, consented to brave the dangers of the gay Rue Bassano. But when Mademoiselle hinted at the horrid possibility that Monsieur Bouchard might be beguiled into sowing a late crop of wild oats, suddenly a grin flashed for a moment on Pierre's stolid countenance — flashed and disappeared so instantly that Mademoiselle Bouchard was not sure he grinned at all. If he did, however, it must have been at the notion that the staid, the correct Monsieur Bouchard could ever sow wild oats. Mademoiselle Celeste blushed faintly

at the thought that she reckoned such
a thing possible.

Pierre then backed out of the door,
wiping two imaginary tears from his

eyes. Once outside with the door
shut, this miscreant did a very strange
thing. He stood on one leg, whirled
around with the greatest agility for his
years, and softly whispered, "Houp
là !"

Papa Bouchard

That very day came the moving. The van arrived, and Monsieur Bouchard's books, papers and clothes were put into it by Pierre, who seemed to be in the deepest dejection. Mademoiselle gave him minute and tearful directions about Monsieur Paul's diet, exercise and clothing. He was to see that Monsieur Paul kept regular hours, and was to report in the Rue Clarisse the smallest infraction of the rules of living which might occur in the Rue Bassano; and Pierre promised with a fervor and glibness that would have excited the suspicions of any one less kindly and simple-minded than good old Mademoiselle. He did indeed awaken a host of doubts in the mind of his faithful Élise, who had not been married for thirty years without finding out a few things about men. And when he wept at telling her good-bye for a single day, she told him not to be shedding any of those crocodile tears around her.

Pierre, mounted on the van that

Papa Bouchard

carried away Monsieur Bouchard's belongings, drove off, looking as melancholy as he could ; but as soon as he turned the corner he began whistling so merrily that the driver asked him if his uncle had n't died and left him some money.

When the Rue Bassano was reached Pierre jumped down and skipped up stairs with the agility of twenty instead of fifty. He was as charmed with Monsieur's new apartment as Monsieur himself had been. It was so intensely modern. Light everywhere — all sorts of new-fashioned conveniences — nothing in the least like the dismal old Rue Clarisse. And the view from the windows — so very gay ! And the noise — so delicious, so intoxicatingly interesting ! The sound of rag time music came from the two music halls across the way. Pierre, dropping all pretence of work, was inspired to do the *can-can*, whistling and singing meanwhile. The open window proved

Papa Bouchard

so attractive that Pierre spent a good part of the time hanging out of it, and only by fits and starts got Monsieur Bouchard's belongings in place. And the more he saw of the place, the more exuberant was his delight with it, and the more determined he was to stay there. The last tenant — the jolly young journalist named Marsac — had left, as Monsieur Bouchard had noted, some souvenirs on the walls in the shape of gaudy posters and brilliant chromos of ballet girls. These, Pierre might be expected to remove when he began to hang on the walls the severely classic pictures that constituted Monsieur Bouchard's collection of art. But Pierre seemed to know by clairvoyance Monsieur Bouchard's latent tastes. He hung " The Coliseum by Moonlight " — a very fine etching — immediately under a red-and-gold young lady who was making a quarter past six with her dainty, uplifted toe. " Socrates and His Pupils " were put where they could get an admirable view of another red-and-gold young lady who was making twelve o'clock meridian as nearly as a human being could. "Kittens at Play" — a great favorite of Mademoiselle's — was side by side with a picture of Courier, who won the Grand Prix that year, and a very noble portrait of President Loubet was placed next a cut of a celebrated English prize fighter, stripped for the ring. The remainder of the things were neatly arranged; the *concièrge*, who was to supply Monsieur Bouchard's meals, was interviewed, and an appetizing dinner ordered. Then Pierre, taking possession of the evening newspaper and also of a very comfortable chair by the window, awaited Monsieur Bouchard's arrival.

It was a charming evening in the middle of June, and still broad daylight at seven o'clock. But Pierre, presently lighting a lamp and drawing the shades, gave the apartment a homelike and inviting aspect.

24

Papa Bouchard

Just as the clock struck seven Monsieur Bouchard's step was heard on the stair. Seven o'clock had been Monsieur Bouchard's hour of coming home since he was fifteen years old, and he had never varied from it three minutes in thirty-seven years. He entered the drawing-room with a new and jovial air, but when he saw Pierre his countenance turned as black as a thunder-cloud.

"What are you doing here?" he asked, curtly.

"I came, Monsieur, by Mademoiselle's orders," civilly replied Pierre.

"Mademoiselle's orders" was still a phrase to conjure by with Monsieur Bouchard. When the yoke of forty years is thrown off there is still a feeling as if it were bearing on the neck. Monsieur Bouchard threw his gloves crossly on the table and asked for his dinner.

"It will be here in five minutes, Monsieur," replied Pierre. "Will not

25

Papa Bouchard

Monsieur look about the apartment and see if I have arranged things to suit him ?   The pictures, for example ? "

Monsieur, still sulky, rose, and the first thing his eye fell on was the prize fighter's portrait under President Loubet's.

" This is intolerable ! " he said, indignantly.   " Why did n't you take this prize-fighting daub down ? "

" Because," readily responded Pierre, " the place where it was would be marked on the wall; and besides, I did not like to take the liberty without Monsieur's permission."

Monsieur Bouchard passed on to the next picture, that of the hero of the Grand Prix.   He liked horses — in pictures, that is — and really found Courier more to his taste than " Kittens at Play."   His countenance cleared, and when Pierre gravely directed him to the young lady poised on one toe and reaching skyward with the other, a faint smile actually ap-

Papa Bouchard

peared on Monsieur Bouchard's face.
Then, his eye falling on the other young
lady who was trying to make twelve
o'clock meridian, every wrinkle on his
forehead smoothed out, his mouth came
open like a rat trap, and he involunta-
rily assumed an attitude of pleased contemplation, with his hands under his
coat tails.

Suddenly, however, it flashed on him
that Mademoiselle Bouchard's paid detective, in the person of Pierre, was
eyeing him, and with the quickness of
thought Monsieur Bouchard's apprecia-
tive smile gave way to a portentous
frown, and turning to Pierre, he said,
sternly :

"Take this thing away! It is reprehensible both in art and morals! I
can't have it here!"

But, wonder of wonders! there
stood Pierre, his mouth wide open in
a silent guffaw, his left eye nearly
closed. Was it possible he was
daring to wink at his master? Pierre,

however, pretty soon solved the situation by putting his finger on the
side of his nose — a shocking familiarity — and say-
ing, roguishly :

"Ah, sir, I have something to say
to you. I was forced, yes, actually
driven, from the decorous quiet of the
Rue Clarisse and the company of Mademoiselle Bouchard and my worthy
Élise and the cats, to this gay locality

Papa Bouchard

by my solicitude for Monsieur. That
is to say, Mademoiselle thinks I was.
One thing is certain — I was sent here
to take care of Monsieur. Well, it
depends entirely on Monsieur how I
take care of him. Do you understand,
sir?"

"N—n—not exactly." Monsieur
Bouchard was a little frightened. Having Pierre to mount guard over him
seemed destructive of the harmless
liberty and mild gaiety he had promised
himself in the Rue Bassano.

"Just this, sir. My wife, I have
reason to know, expects Monsieur to
watch me and report to her. Mademoiselle expects me to watch Monsieur
and report to *her*. Now, what pre-
vents us from each giving a good account of the other, and meanwhile
doing as we please?"

Monsieur for a moment looked indignant at this impudent proposition,
coming, too, as it did from a servant
whom he had known as the pattern of

29

decorum for thirty years. But only
for a moment. Was it strange, after
all, that thirty years of the Rue Clarisse had bred a spirit of revolt in

this hitherto obedient husband and
submissive servant?

Pierre, seeing evidences of yielding
on the part of Monsieur, proceeded to
clinch the matter.

30

Papa Bouchard

"You see, sir, I found out you were looking at this apartment. If I had told Mademoiselle what I knew about it there 'd have been a pretty kettle of fish. I doubt if Monsieur would have got away from the Rue Clarisse alive. But I did n't. I concluded the Rue Bassano was a very pleasant place to live. I like the lively tunes they play at the music halls across the street, and that theatre round the corner is convenient. But I never should have got away if I had showed how much I wanted to come. When Mademoiselle proposed it to me, I lied like a trooper. I not only lied, but I cried, at the prospect of leaving the Rue Clarisse. That settled it. A woman is like a pig. If you want to drive her to Orleans, you must head her for Strasburg. So here we are, sir, and if we don't have a livelier time here than we did in the Rue Clarisse it will be Monsieur's fault, not mine."

Monsieur met this outrageous speech

by saying, "You are the most impudent, scandalous, scheming, hypocritical
rascal I ever met ——"

Pierre just then heard sounds in the
little lobby which he understood. He
ran out and returned with a tray, which
he placed on the table, already laid for
one. Then, arranging the dishes with
a great flourish, he invited Monsieur
Bouchard to take his place at the table.
Monsieur complied. The first course
was oysters — at three francs the dozen.
Then there was turtle soup; devilled
lobster, duckling *à la Bordelaise* — both
of which were forbidden in the Rue
Clarisse, because Monsieur Bouchard
at the age of seven had been made
ill by them — and a bottle of champagne, a wine that Mademoiselle had
always told her brother was poison to
every member of his family.

But Monsieur Bouchard seemed to
forget all about this. He ate and
drank these things as if he had forgotten all his painful experiences of forty-

32

five years before and as if he had been
brought up on champagne.

It was rather pleasant — this first
quaff of liberty — having what he liked
to eat and drink, and even to wear.
He privately determined before finish-
ing his dinner that he would get a new
tailor next day and have some clothes
made in the latest fashion.

"Have you found out the names of
any persons in the house?" asked Monsieur after dinner, lighting a cigar. It
was his second; in the Rue Clarisse
he was limited to one.

"No one at all, sir," replied that
double-dyed villain, Pierre. "It is n't
judicious to know all sorts of people.
I intend to forget some I know."

Monsieur Bouchard turned in his
chair and looked at Pierre; the fellow
really seemed changed into another
man from what he had been for thirty
years. But to Monsieur Bouchard the
change was not displeasing. He felt
a bond between himself and Pierre,

3   33

stronger in the last half-hour than in the thirty years they had been master and man. They exchanged looks — it might even be said winks — and Monsieur Bouchard poured out another glass of champagne — his third. And what with the wine and the dinner, he was in that state of exhilaration which the sense of liberty newly acquired always brings.

"Monsieur won't want me any more to-night?" asked Pierre.

"No," replied Monsieur Bouchard, "but — be sure to be here at —" he meant to say at ten o'clock that night, but changed his mind and said, "seven o'clock to-morrow morning."

"Certainly, sir," answered Pierre. "I expect to be home and in bed before three."

And he said this with such a debonair manner that Monsieur Bouchard was secretly charmed, and privately determined to acquire something of the same tone.

Papa Bouchard

Pierre gone, Monsieur Bouchard made himself comfortable in an easy-chair and began toying with a fourth cigar. How agreeable were these modern apartments, after all — everything furnished, every want anticipated — all a tenant had to do was to walk in and hang up his hat. Then his thoughts wandered to that very pretty woman who had travelled in the same train with him that day to St. Germains, and the day before to Verneuil, whither he had gone to look after some property of Léontine's. Madame Vernet was her name — it was on her travelling bag — and she was a widow — that fact had leaked out ten seconds after he met her. But she was so very demure, so modest, not to say bashful, that she seemed more like a nun than a widow. And so timid — everything frightened her. She trembled when the guard asked her for her ticket, and clung quite desperately to Monsieur Bouchard's arm in the station at Ver-

Papa Bouchard

neuil. She had expected her aunt and
uncle to meet her, and when they were
not to be found, blushingly accepted
Monsieur Bouchard's services in getting
a cab. And that day, on stepping into
the railway carriage to go to St. Germains, there was the dear little diffident
thing again. She was charmed to see
her friend of the day before, and ex-
plained that she was to spend the day
with another uncle and aunt she had
living at St. Germains. Knowing her
inability to care for herself in a crowd,
Monsieur Bouchard had meant to put
her into a cab, as he had done the day
before. But just as the train stopped
he was seized by a couple of snuffy old
antiquarians and hustled off by them
before he could even offer to take
charge of the quiet, the retiring, the
clinging and helpless Madame Vernet.

Monsieur Bouchard lay back in his
chair recalling her prim but pretty gray
gown, her fleecy veil of gray gauze, that
covered but did not conceal her charm-

36

ing features, and her extremely natty boots. He could not for the life of him remember whether he had mentioned to her on their first meeting that he was going to St. Germains next day. While he was cogitating this point he was rudely disturbed by the opening of the door, and Captain de Meneval walked in briskly.

Now, this good-looking captain of artillery, who had married Monsieur Bouchard's ward, Léontine, was not exactly to Monsieur's taste. It is true he had never been able to find out anything to de Meneval's discredit — and he had looked pretty closely into the captain's affairs at the time of Léontine's marriage. As for Léontine herself, she was devoted to her captain and always represented him as being the kindest as well as the most agreeable of husbands. True, he was always complaining about the modest income that Papa Bouchard allowed them, but Léontine herself was ever doing that, and urged de Meneval

37

on in his complaints. Monsieur Bouchard was a little annoyed at de Meneval's entrance, especially as the artillery
captain had adopted a hail-fellow-well-
met air, highly objectionable on the
part of a man toward another man who
practically holds the purse-strings for
number one.

Therefore, Monsieur Bouchard rather
stiffly gave Captain de Meneval three
fingers and offered him a chair.

"Changed your quarters, eh?" said
de Meneval, looking about him.
"Found the Rue Clarisse rather slow,
and came off here where you can be
your own man, so to speak?"

"I was not actuated by any such
motive," coldly replied Monsieur Bouchard. "I came here because the rooms
I had in the Rue Clarisse were cramped,
and I needed to have more space, as
well as to be in a more convenient quarter of Paris."

De Meneval's bright eyes had been
travelling round the walls, and Monsieur

Papa Bouchard

Bouchard remembered, with cold chills running up and down his back, the pictures of his predecessor — that scampish young journalist, Marsac — so indiscreetly left hanging by Pierre. A shout of laughter from de Meneval, and a pointing of his stick toward the red-and-gold young ladies, showed Monsieur Bouchard that his apprehensions were not unfounded.

"Is that your selection, Papa Bouchard?" cried the reprobate captain. "Never saw them before — you must have kept them in hiding in the Rue Clarisse. I'll tell Léontine," and the captain laughed loudly.

He had a great haw-haw of a laugh that had always been particularly annoying to Monsieur Bouchard, and this thing of calling him "Papa" Bouchard was an unwarrantable liberty. So he replied, freezingly:

"You are altogether mistaken. These extraordinary prints were left here by my predecessor, a very wild

young journalist — I believe most young
journalists are very wild — and they
come down to-morrow. It would seriously disturb me to have those ballet
pictures around."

"Well, now," said de Meneval, with
an unabashed front, "I think you are
too hard on the poor girls. I have
known a good many of them in my life
— taken them to little suppers, you
know — and generally they're very
hard-working, decent girls. Some of
them have a husband and children to
help to support. Others have dependent parents. They're unconventional
— very — and like to eat and drink at
somebody else's expense, but that's no
great harm. Plenty of other people in
much higher walks of life do the same."

"I don't care to discuss ballet girls
with you, Monsieur de Meneval," remarked Monsieur Bouchard, with great
dignity.

"But I want to discuss them with
you," answered de Meneval, with what

Papa Bouchard

Monsieur Bouchard thought most improper levity and familiarity. "That's what I came to you this evening about. That's why I have been haunting the Rue Clarisse during the last ten days, trying to see you alone."

"Yes. I know that I have been honored with a good many cards of yours. Also of Léontine's."

" Oh, Léontine ! You may be sure she does not come on the errand that brings me. While she feels the narrowness of our income as much as I do, she manages to live within her allowance, and I don't believe owes a franc in the world. But, Papa Bouchard, to come to business ——"

De Meneval paused. He had a good deal of courage, but the stony silence with which his confidences were met would have disconcerted an ogre.

" Go on, Monsieur le Capitaine," said Monsieur Bouchard, icily.

" I'm going on. You see, it is just this way — that is —" de Meneval

floundered — " as I was going to say —
Léontine, you know, is perfect — it
really is touching to see how she bears
our enforced but unnecessary poverty.
I wish I could do as well."

Here de Meneval came to a dead
stop, and Monsieur Bouchard, by way
of encouraging him, repeated, in the
same tone :

" Go on, Monsieur le Capitaine."

" But I *can't* go on with you fixing
that basilisk glare on me," cried de
Meneval, rising and walking about
excitedly. " I believe, if you say, ' Go
on, Monsieur le Capitaine,' to me again,
I 'll do something desperate — smash
the mirror with my stick, or turn on
the fire alarm. I assure you, Monsieur Bouchard, I am still a respectable member of society. I don't beat
my wife or cheat at cards, and I have
never committed a felony in my life."

" Glad to hear it," was Papa Bouchard's fatherly reception of this speech.

De Meneval, after walking once or

twice up and down the room, succeeded in mastering his indignation,
and sat quietly down in the chair he
had just vacated, facing Monsieur Bouchard, and then, still floundering awkwardly, managed to say :

"I — I — am very much in want
— I am, at present — in short, I am in
the most unpleasant predicament." And
then he mumbled, " Money."

" So I knew the moment you entered this room," was Monsieur Bouchard's rejoinder.

" Then, sir," said de Meneval, re-
covering his spirits now that the murder
was out, " I wish you had said so in
the beginning. It would have saved
me a very bad quarter of an hour."

"Young man," severely replied
Monsieur Bouchard, " I had not the
slightest wish to save you a bad quarter
of an hour."

" So it seems; but I will tell you
just how it stands. You know I am
stationed at Melun —— "

Papa Bouchard

"I have known that fact ever since I knew you."

"Very well, sir. There is a music hall at Melun — the Pigeon House — with a garden back of it, kept by one Michaux, a rascal, if ever I saw one. Now, it's very dull at Melun the evenings I am on duty and can't get back to Léontine in Paris, and it's a small place, and quite naturally, when one hears the music going at the Pigeon House, and sees the lights flashing and the people eating and drinking under the trees on the terrace garden, it's quite natural, I say, to drop in there for the evening."

"Quite natural for you, sir. Go on, Monsieur le Capitaine."

De Meneval restrained his impulse to brain Monsieur Bouchard, sitting so sternly and primly before him, and kept on:

"Then there is the garden — jolly place, with electric lights — where you can get a pretty fair meal. It is quite

44

And the girls are permitted to come out in their stage costumes, to have an ice or a glass of wine.

unique — nothing like it in Paris or anywhere else that I can think of, and I've seen a good many — " here de Meneval hastily checked himself. " It's quite the thing to give suppers to the young ladies of the ballet — and some of them are not so young, either — in the gardens. The proprietor, of course, encourages it, and the girls are permitted to come out in their stage costumes to have an ice or a glass of wine. All the fellows in my regiment do it; it's considered quite the thing, and their mothers and sisters come out to the Pigeon House to see them do it. If it was n't for the support given the place by the garrison it would have to close up, and then Melun would be duller than ever. The Pigeon House is unconventional, but perfectly respectable."

" Possibly," drily replied Monsieur Bouchard, " but not probably."

" Good heavens, sir! you are mistaken. Léontine has been teasing me for a month past to take her out there to supper some evening, and I 've promised to do so this very next week. Do you think I 'd take my wife to any place that was n't respectable ? "

De Meneval was getting warm over this, and Monsieur Bouchard was forced to admit that he supposed the Pigeon House *was* respectable.

" But that does n't prevent these jolly little suppers to the young ladies of the ballet, and especially those given to them by the officers. I assure you it is mere harmless eating and drinking. The poor girls have to work hard, and when they get through of an evening I dare say very few of them have two francs to buy something to eat. So a number of us have got into the way of giving these poor souls supper after the performance. Even Major Fallière goes to these suppers, and you know his nickname in the regiment."

" No, I know of him only as a very correct, middle-aged man. I wish you had the same sort of reputation as Major Fallière."

"Well, he is called by the juniors old P. M. P. — that is to say, the Pink of Military Propriety. And Fallière is my chum, and *he* goes to these little suppers."

De Meneval brought this out with an air of triumph, but Monsieur Bouchard remained coldly unresponsive, and then de Meneval let the cat out of the bag.

"And I say, Monsieur Bouchard, the proprietor of the Pigeon House sent me in my account the other day — nineteen hundred francs nineteen centimes — and I have n't got the money to pay it."

De Meneval lay back and waited for the explosion. Monsieur Bouchard started from his chair, bawling:

"Nineteen hundred francs! And you no doubt expect me to pay it out of your wife's income! I wonder what Léontine would say to this!"

Papa Bouchard

" That's just what I 've been wondering, too," replied de Meneval, somewhat dolefully. " Léontine is the dearest girl in the world, but she is a
woman, after all. I can prove to her
that I have never given a franc's worth
to any other woman, except something
to eat and drink, but all the same I 'd
just as soon she would think I spent
my Melun evenings sitting in my quarters, with her picture before me and
reading up on ballistics, as an artillery
officer should."

" And would you deliberately impose
on her innocence in this respect ? "
asked Monsieur Bouchard, indignantly.

" My dear sir," calmly replied de
Meneval, " you have never been married. If you had, you would not talk
about a man's imposing on his wife's
innocence. Love is clairvoyant, and
most men know what their wives wish
to believe, and gratify them accordingly.
It 's a very complex subject, and needs
to be dealt with intelligently."

Papa Bouchard

"I think our standard of intelligence is not the same," grimly responded Monsieur Bouchard. "But when I tell Léontine about this nineteen hundred francs due at the Pigeon House, I trust she will be able to deal with you intelligently."

"I am afraid she will," replied de Meneval, with some anxiety; "but after it's paid I know I can persuade her that it was not the least actual harm — just a little lark in the way of killing time."

"And may I ask, since you speak so confidently of its being paid, whom do you expect to pay it?"

"You, sir, of course," replied de Meneval, taking a cigar out of Monsieur Bouchard's case.

Papa Bouchard jumped as if a hornet had stung him. "I, sir? Since you have assumed this modest expectation, perhaps you anticipate that I will pay it out of my private income?"

"Oh, no, I mean out of my wife's

income," replied de Meneval, puffing away at his cigar.

"You are too modest, Monsieur le Capitaine. Now let me tell you this — you misunderstood your customer in bringing this outrageous bill to me, and it won't be paid. I have a sincere affection for Léontine, and I don't intend to let any captain of artillery in the French army, husband or no husband, make ducks and drakes of her money."

Papa Bouchard leaned back, folded his arms and looked the embodiment of statuesque determination. Captain de Meneval puffed a while longer at his cigar, and then rose. There was resolution, as if he still held a trump card to play, written on his countenance.

"Very well, Monsieur Bouchard," he said, readjusting the blossom in his buttonhole. "I am sorry you are so unyielding. You didn't ask me if I was prepared to offer any security that the loan would be repaid. If you had I should have given you this."

Papa Bouchard

De Meneval pulled from his pocket a glittering string of diamonds, every stone glittering like a star.

"This is the diamond necklace I gave Léontine on our marriage. Of

course, I could not afford it, but I was in love with her — I'm more in love with her now — and I gave her what would please her, without counting the cost."

Papa Bouchard gasped. "And Léontine — does she know of this?"

Papa Bouchard

De Meneval shook his head. "You
see, when I bought this necklace for
forty thousand francs the jeweller
showed me at the same time an exact
copy of it in paste — seventy-five
francs. He told me when he sold a
necklace like this he usually sold a coun-
terfeit, for emergencies — you know.
I bought the seventy-five franc necklace, too — and I did n't mention it
to Léontine. I think all the philoso-
phers, beginning with the Egyptian
school of something or other B. C.,
down through the Greeks and the Ro-
mans to Kant and Schopenhauer, agree
that it is not philosophic for a married man to tell everything to his wife.
So I never told Léontine about this
imitation necklace, but kept it for an
emergency, as the jeweller — a married man — advised me. To-night,
when I saw I was in a tight place and
had to come to you, I quietly slipped
the paste necklace into the case, which
we keep in our strong-box, and put the

54

real one into my pocket. I came within an ace of being caught by Léontine, though. The dear girl entered the room a minute afterward and asked me to get out her diamond necklace — she was going to the opera with some friends of hers — and off she's gone, glittering with paste, and as innocent as a lamb, while here is the real thing."

Papa Bouchard was staggered for a minute or two. Then he said: "So you expected me to turn amateur pawnbroker for your benefit?"

"Well," replied de Meneval, stroking his moustache, "I should not have put it in that brutally frank fashion myself, but if you don't care to act the amateur pawnbroker, I shall be obliged to take it to the professionals."

"No, no, no," cried Papa Bouchard. He really was fond of Léontine, and didn't mean to risk her diamonds. Nevertheless, there was a stand-and-

55

deliver air about the whole transaction which vexed him inexpressibly. He sat silent for a while and so did de Meneval.

Papa Bouchard, for all that he had been hectored by a woman all his life, was yet no fool. He saw that de Meneval had him in a trap, and reasoned out the whole thing inside of two minutes.

" Now, Monsieur le Capitaine," he said, presently, " I see where we stand. I will not lend you the money out of Léontine's income — but I will lend it to you myself. I shall keep this necklace until the money is paid. Meanwhile, I shall go out to see this place — the Pigeon House — and judge for myself all these facts that you allege."

" Do ! " cried the cheerful reprobate, with a grin. " Perhaps you'll like it and get into the habit of going there."

" And perhaps," replied Papa Bouchard, " I may not like it, and you may have your income reduced if you

Papa Bouchard

persist in going there. And then —
when the whole transaction is concluded and the money repaid, I shall
disclose every particular of it to Léontine."

"By all means!" De Meneval was
actually laughing in Papa Bouchard's
face. "I'll deny every word of it, of
course, and call for proof. I'll tell
Léontine you tried to persuade me to
go out there with you and I refused.
I'll say *you* gave the suppers, and I'll
bring twenty of the best fellows in the
regiment to swear to it — and you'll see
who comes out ahead in *that* game."

Papa Bouchard was so horrified at
the cold-blooded villainy of this that
he could hardly speak for a minute.
But he refused to take the threat seriously, and demanding the bill, which
de Meneval promptly produced, said,
stiffly:

"You will hear from me in a day or
two."

"And how about the advance?"

57

Papa Bouchard

asked de Meneval, "I should like about a thousand francs in cash."

Papa Bouchard put up his eye-glass and surveyed Captain de Meneval all over, which scrutiny was borne with the greatest coolness by the brazen captain of artillery.

"You see," continued de Meneval, "the story is very liable to get into the newspapers — *extremely* liable, I may say. It will be something like this — that Monsieur Bouchard held Captain and Madame de Meneval so tight that they were compelled to let Monsieur Bouchard have Madame's diamond necklace for a small loan — and the newspapers will probably make it out to be Léontine's wardrobe and my watch and chain besides."

De Meneval paused — the fellow knew when to stop. Monsieur Bouchard, swelling with rage, paused too — and then, taking out his cheque book, angrily wrote a cheque for a thousand francs, which he handed Captain de

Papa Bouchard

Meneval in exchange for a sheaf of bills produced by the captain.

"Before paying another franc, I shall go out to the Pigeon House and investigate the whole business," said Monsieur Bouchard, savagely.

"Ta, ta!" called out the graceless dog of a captain, picking up his hat. "Remember, you are on your good behavior. One single indiscretion at the Pigeon House and I'll telegraph the whole story to Mademoiselle Bouchard, and then —— "

Papa Bouchard simply sat and swelled the more with rage at the unabashed front of this captain of artillery — but he was galvanized into motion by a light tap on the door and a musical voice calling:

"Are you in, Papa Bouchard?"

Although all the fulminations of Monsieur Bouchard had failed to affect

Papa Bouchard

Captain de Meneval, the sound of that voice flurried him considerably. For it was Léontine's, and de Meneval had no particular desire for an interview with her under Papa Bouchard's basilisk eye. He turned quite pale, did this robust captain, and muttered :

" I don't want to be caught here."

Papa Bouchard smiled in a superior manner — he rather liked the notion of de Meneval being caught there — and called out to Léontine :

" Come in."

M. Bouchard's hat, cape-greatcoat and umbrella lay on a chair where he had placed them on coming in. Without so much as saying, " By your leave," de Meneval slung the greatcoat round him, clapped Papa Bouchard's hat on his head, seized the umbrella in such a way as to hide his face, and with his own hat under his arm opened the door to the lobby and darted past Léontine, nearly knocking her down.

Papa Bouchard

Léontine, wearing an evening gown, a long and beautiful white mantle, and a chiffon scarf over her head, entered, somewhat discomposed by her encounter.

"What a very rude man that was who pushed by me so suddenly!" she said, advancing. "Some of your tiresome clients, Papa Bouchard, and I order you not to have that creature here again." And she ran forward and kissed Papa Bouchard on his bald head.

Now, it was plain that this pretty Léontine took liberties with her guardian, godfather and trustee, and also that Papa Bouchard liked these liberties. It was in vain that he tried to assume a stern air with Léontine. She pinched his ear when he scolded, drew caricatures of him when he frowned, and when at last he was forced to smile, as he always was, perched herself on the arm of his chair and declined to be evicted. And she

Papa Bouchard

was so very pretty! The French have
a saying that the devil himself was
handsome when he was young. Léontine de Meneval had more than the
mere beauty of youth, of form, of
color. She was the em-
bodiment of graceful gaiety.
She looked like one of those
brilliant white butterflies
whose lives are spent dancing in the sun. The great
and glorious dowry of love,
of youth, of beauty, of
health, of happiness was
hers. Her entering the
room was like a breath of
daffodils in spring. She
was a most beguiling creature. It was a source of wonder and
congratulation to Papa Bouchard that
this charming girl did not succeed in
bamboozling all of her own income
out of him and all of his as well.

Having kissed him, pinched his ear,
and otherwise agreeably maltreated

Papa Bouchard

her trustee, Léontine looked round the
new apartment with dancing eyes.

"Well," she cried, laughing, "I see
how it is. You could n't stand the
Rue Clarisse another day or hour. Did
anybody ever tell you, Papa Bouchard,
that you had a vein of — a vein of —
what shall I call it? — a taste for the
wine of life in you?"

"Nobody ever did," replied Papa
Bouchard, trying to be stern.

"Then I tell you so. And look at
these pictures — oh, oh!"

Léontine covered her face with her
chiffon scarf, to avoid the sight of the
young ladies pointing skyward with
their toes.

"And I wonder what Aunt Céleste
will say when she sees them," continued
this impish Léontine.

"She won't see them. They will
be removed to-morrow," hastily put in
Papa Bouchard.

"You 'd better, you dear old thing,
if you value your life. I shall have to

63

Papa Bouchard

tell Victor about this. How he will
laugh! I do all I can to make him
laugh and to amuse him when he is
with me, for it is *so* dull for him when
he is obliged to stay at Melun. When
his regimental duties are over he has
nothing to do in the evening but to
sit in his quarters and study up ballistics, as he calls it, and look at my
picture by way of refreshment."

Papa Bouchard sniffed. He commonly sniffed at the mention of Captain
de Meneval's name.

" But," continued Léontine, trying
to curl Papa Bouchard's scanty hair,
using her pretty fingers for curling
tongs, " he won't be so lonely now at
Melun, for his old chum, Major Fallière, is stationed there, too, and he and
Victor are like brothers. You know,
dear Papa Bouchard, that you yourself
admitted Major Fallière's friendship to
be a letter of recommendation to any
man. He is called the Pink of Military Propriety, and if Victor led the

64

Papa Bouchard

larky life you so unjustly suspect him
of, he could n't be friends with Major
Fallière, who is positively straitlaced."

"I can't say I ever saw a really
straitlaced major," replied Papa Bouchard.

"And I have not yet seen this dear
old P. M. P. He was in Algiers when
Victor and I were married — and he
has been so little in Paris since his return that he has not yet had a chance
to call. But he has sent me word by
Victor that he already loves me, and I
hope to see him in a few days, for Victor has promised to let me come out to
Melun and dine at the Pigeon House."

"The Pigeon House!"

"Yes. Why not? You'll be going
there yourself, I dare say, now that you
have eloped from Aunt Céleste. Oh,
you'll be a desperate character in time,
I have no doubt. I see it in your eye.
Victor and I, though, shall keep watch
on you, if you go too far and too
fast!"

Papa Bouchard

This was a nice way for a ward to talk to her trustee — and such a trustee as Monsieur Bouchard! Therefore Papa Bouchard called up his most resolute air of disapproval, and said:

"I am afraid the Pigeon House is hardly a proper place for you to go to, Léontine."

"If I thought that I should have been out there long ago," responded this sprightly imp. "But, unluckily, it's perfectly proper."

"I wish," replied Papa Bouchard, "you could get one single serious idea into that head of yours."

"I have a great many serious ideas," said Léontine, suddenly assuming an unwonted air of gravity, and leaving her perch on the arm of Papa Bouchard's chair for a seat directly facing him. "What would you say if I told you that I am taking a deep and real interest in practical sociological questions, such as giving employment to the deserving workers?"

66

Papa Bouchard

" I should say you were at least reaching the development I have always
wished for you. But I hope you are
confining your experiments to giving
work only. The mere giving of money
tends to pauperize. The giving of
work is the intelligent mode of benefit-
ing a man or a woman."

"That's it precisely," cried Léontine,
instantly losing her air of gravity, and
jumping up to kiss the bald spot on the
top of Papa Bouchard's head. Then
she resumed her chair and her serious
manner simultaneously. " That's what
I knew you'd say, dear Papa Bouchard.
I had your approval in mind all the
time. It came about in this way," continued Léontine, solemnly. " There
is a very worthy man — a Pole, Putzki
by name — who is one of the best
tailors in Paris. I became very much
interested in this man ; likewise in his
jackets, coats and riding habits. I have
been to his shop several times and
talked with him. The man is an exile

from his native country. How sad
that is! And he cannot go back. He
is very deserving and has a family to
support. He doesn't ask for charity,
but I gave him —— "

"All the money you had," hastily and
angrily interjected Papa Bouchard.

"Not at all," replied Léontine, with
dignity. "I had learned better than
that. I have not given him a franc.
But I ordered, out of pure charity and
good will to a fellow creature, five
walking gowns, three jackets, two long
coats, a yachting costume and a couple
of riding habits."

Papa Bouchard's mouth opened wide,
but no sound came forth. Léontine,
taking advantage of his amazed silence,
kept on, rapidly:

"Then there is another deserving
case — Louise, a milliner and modiste.
She has a husband who squanders her
money on his pleasures. If Victor did
that I think it would kill me. Like
Putzki she does not ask money, but

work. Out of sympathy for her, I have had her make me four ball gowns, nine visiting and house costumes, some little négligées and things, and about eighteen hats. And here are the bills."

With this Léontine drew out two huge bills and thrust them into Papa Bouchard's scowling face. Not only was he annoyed with Léontine for her extravagance, but he was conscious that she had fooled him. He sat perfectly still and silent, glaring into Léontine's serious, pretty countenance — not so serious, though, but that Papa Bouchard saw the shadow of a smile on her rose-lipped mouth.

"And you expect to pay those bills out of your allowance, I presume?" said Papa Bouchard, sarcastically, after a moment.

"You flatter me," replied Léontine. "I always knew I was a good financier, but to expect me to pay such bills as these out of my meagre allowance is

69

to credit me with the financial genius of a Rothschild."

"Then they will go unpaid!" cried Papa Bouchard, determinedly. This assault on him, following hard on Captain de Meneval's, was rather more than he could stand. Léontine did not know it, but the defeat Papa Bouchard had just suffered at the hands of that good-looking scapegrace, her husband, had hardened his heart against her and her milliner's and tailor's bills. However, she was not easily frightened. She only tapped her little foot, smiled loftily and said:

"But they *must* be paid!"

Papa Bouchard, who had no more voice than a crow, began to hum a tune and to turn over the leaves of a scientific journal that lay on the table before him. A pause followed. Then Léontine said again, very softly and very determinedly:

"And they *will* be paid."

"How, may I ask?" inquired Papa

Papa Bouchard

Bouchard, whirling round on her. Léontine, throwing aside her chiffon scarf, which she had held round her bare, white neck, showed a string of diamonds, as she thought them to be — paste, Papa Bouchard knew them to be — and said:

" My wedding gift from Victor. They are worth forty thousand francs. I can easily raise ten thousand on them."

Papa Bouchard lay back in his chair, absolutely stunned. So, both of them were for turning the necklace into cash! And what scandal would be precipitated if Léontine carried out her intention! The necklace would be discovered to be paste, and Léontine would naturally be deeply incensed against her husband; Papa Bouchard was that already, but he really loved his little Léontine, and the thought of trouble between her and her husband disturbed him.

" Does Captain de Meneval know of these bills?" he asked, significantly.

Papa Bouchard

Léontine hung her head. " No," she faltered, " and that is the part which distresses me. Victor has been so *very* prudent — has no bills, poor fellow — he has no amusements away from me — and I — I have been so self-

ish —" Léontine's eyes were bright with tears.

" Don't make yourself unhappy about Victor being too prudent. He need never give you any anxiety on that point," was Papa Bouchard's unfeeling reply.

There was a moment's silence. Papa

Papa Bouchard

Bouchard, who had a shrewd head for business, was rapidly cogitating the best thing to do under the circumstances. Léontine, who had no head for business at all, was wondering how she could keep Victor from noticing the absence of the necklace. She had just concluded to fall into a state of great weakness and prostration, thus preventing her from going into society, when she received something like a galvanic shock, for there, before her eyes, Papa Bouchard was holding up the exact counterpart of her necklace. The two necklaces made a blaze of light.

" Where did you get it ? " she gasped, pointing to the glittering thing in Papa Bouchard's hand.

Now, Papa Bouchard was a clever man, as men are clever, but he was not so clever as a woman. A brilliant scheme had flashed into his mind — he would produce the real necklace, tell Léontine it was paste, and so make sure that she would not take it to the

73

pawnbroker; and he could manage both
de Meneval and Léontine equally well
with the paste necklace. He did not
much fancy having the responsibility
of so many diamonds as the real one
contained. But he had not foreseen
this direct and embarrassing question of
Léontine's. He looked blank for a
moment or two, and then, having no
better answer ready, replied testily:

"I wish you wouldn't ask such questions, Léontine. Of course I came
by it honestly."

"Of course—of course," cried Léontine, jumping up. "Does Aunt Céleste know of this?"

"N—n—no," faltered Papa Bouchard. This was another facer for
him.

Léontine had not the slightest doubt
that Papa Bouchard could give a perfectly rational and correct account of
how he came by the necklace — it was
probably the property of some client —
but seeing a fine chance to hold Papa

74

Papa Bouchard

Bouchard up to obloquy and to lecture
him, she promptly determined to give
him the benefit of her pretended suspicions. She therefore rose with great
dignity, gathered her drapery about her,
and looking significantly at Papa Bouchard, said:

"You will pardon me for saying that
this has a most singular appearance,
and I shall lose no time in informing
Aunt Céleste."

Papa Bouchard turned pale. Was
ever such a diabolical trap laid for an
innocent man? He was not at all
sure, if he gave the true account of
how he came by the stones, that Captain de Meneval would not carry out
his threat and deny the whole business.
The fellow had actually laughed while
he was making the threat, and seemed
to regard it as an excellent joke to im-
pair the peace and honor of a respectable elderly gentleman. Papa Bouchard
got up, sat down again, and groaned.

"Léontine," he said, to that professedly indignant young woman, "you don't understand."

"No, I *don't* understand," replied Léontine, with unkind emphasis.

"It was this way — I was out at St. Germains the other day —" Papa Bouchard was floundering hopelessly, but a bright thought struck him — "the day of the meeting of the Society of French Antiquarians. Very interesting time we had — several specimens of the paleozoic age were found ——"

"And this match to my necklace was among them? Fie, Papa Bouchard!"

"Not at all. Will you let me speak? I say I was out at St. Germains for the meeting of the Society of French Antiquarians. The curator of the museum is a great friend of mine — he has an old mother — finest old lady you ever saw — eighty years old, bedridden and stone blind, but as young as a daisy, full of life and talk — it's a treat to see her. My friend wanted a

birthday present for her, and I had seen
this necklace in a shop window in the
Avenue de l'Opéra — and I proposed
to — to — to — " Papa Bouchard faltered.

" Buy it for an old lady, eighty years
old and bedridden? Oh, Papa Bouchard, try again ! "

" Léontine," said Papa Bouchard,
sternly, " I don't like these flippant in-
terruptions. I did not say — I never
meant to say that I proposed to buy
a diamond necklace for an old lady,
bedridden and eighty years of age.
It happened there were spectacles
of all kinds made and kept at the
same shop — and I went and got a
pair of Scotch pebble glasses, at fifty
francs —— "

" But you said she was stone
blind ? "

" What if I did ? I didn't say I
got the glasses for her. But as I see
you won't let me tell you the story of
the necklace, I shall simply keep it to

77

myself. As a matter of fact, they are not diamonds, they are paste."

Léontine, taking the real stones in her hand, examined them carefully. Then, laying them against the necklace around her own milk-white throat, she remarked : " I see they are. Paste, pure and simple."

Papa Bouchard could hardly suppress a smile at this, but he did.

" Very well. They are paste, and they cost seventy-five francs. Now, I will make you a proposition. I propose that I shall look into these bills and see what arrangement can be made with Putzki and Louise, and reach some basis of settlement whereby I may be able, by making a series of small payments out of your income, to get rid of them. Meanwhile, I am afraid to trust you with your own necklace — you will always be trying to raise money on it. So I shall hand you over this paste one, which no one but a jeweller can tell from the real

one. You will give me the real one
— and I will hold it until your bills
are paid. Then I will return it to
you. I suppose you don't wish your
husband to know of this, and I will
agree to keep it from him as long as
you keep out of debt. But if you ever
transgress in this way again I shall tell
him the whole story."

Léontine listened to this with the
utmost gravity, and then replied:
"You are a very clever man, Papa
Bouchard, but you will find your little
Léontine a very clever woman — too
clever to put her head in the noose
you have so kindly held open for her.
I sha'n't dream of giving up my necklace for anything less than a cheque
out of my own money for the payment
in full of these bills. I should be willing to take the paste necklace tempo-
rarily until the bills are paid. After
you have returned it to me I sha'n't
be in the least afraid of your telling
Victor, for if you do I shall tell Aunt

Papa Bouchard

Céleste all your tales about the bedridden old lady and the trip to St. Germains and the widow —— ”

“ What widow ? ” asked Papa Bouchard, forgetful for a moment of the
lady he had met in the railway carriage
two days in succession.

“ The prim little widow you went
to Verneuil with. My maid happened
to be on the same train and saw you
helping her out, and heard you say to
her you were going to St. Germains to-
day — and by the way, I happen to know
you *did* go to St. Germains to-day.”

What a story was this to hatch about
the most correct old gentleman in
Paris ! Papa Bouchard simply glared
at Léontine, but that merry young
woman was smiling and dimpling, as if
debts and duns and trips to Verneuil
and diamond necklaces were quite the
ordinary ingredients of life. The hen
that hatched a cockatrice was no more
puzzled and dismayed than was Papa
Bouchard at the vagaries of his ward.

Papa Bouchard

"Well," cried he, after a pause, determined to put a bold front on the matter, "what if I did find a lady in the same railway carriage with me, going to Verneuil? I had n't hired the whole train, or even a whole carriage. And what if she was a widow, and good-looking! And suppose to-day, in the pursuit of science, I go to St. Germains and quite by accident I find the same lady in the compartment with me? What does that mean except a series of accidents?"

"Yes, a series of accidents," replied Léontine, with an arch glance. The minx seemed to have no more conscience about teasing poor Papa Bouchard than had her rattlebrain of a husband. "It is remarkable that accidents like these always happen in cycles. I should be willing to wager that a third accident is now brewing, and you will see that prim little widow again before the week is out. I should n't be surprised if this change of quarters had something to do with it!"

"Léontine!" said Papa Bouchard, indignantly, but that heedless young person only laughed and said:

"I'll tell Victor that. How the dear boy will laugh! The fact is, I don't know whether I can let Victor associate with you or not — you might lead him off into your own primrose path of dalliance with widows!"

Was ever anything so exasperating! Papa Bouchard ground his teeth — he had a great mind to throw over the whole business of Léontine's money and her affairs, only he knew it would please her too well. His grim meditations were interrupted by Léontine tapping him on the shoulder and saying, "Now, will you hand me over the cheque for the whole amount of those bills — six thousand francs — or must I take this" — touching the paste necklace round her throat — "to the pawnbroker?"

"You certainly can't expect me to

give you a cheque until I have looked into these swindling bills," answered Papa Bouchard.

"I certainly do," tartly said Léontine, "and you will either hand me over immediately a cheque for six thousand francs, or I will drive to Aunt Céleste's before I go to the opera — and I think you 'll have an early visit from her in the morning. I shall tell her about this mysterious necklace, and the pretty widow you have no doubt been running after for at least six months —— "

"I never saw her in my life until yesterday," cried Monsieur Bouchard.

"So you say. Perhaps you have been pursuing her for a year."

Monsieur Bouchard tore his hair, but there was no help for him. After an angry pause, he sat down, wrote out a cheque for six thousand francs, which he slammed down on the table, and Léontine picked up with a joyful cry. And then, with a desperate attempt at an authoritative manner, he said, sternly,

" Pray understand, Léontine, that I reserve the right to tell your husband all the circumstances of this affair if I choose to. I am not intimidated by your threat to tell my sister some cock-and-bull story about *me*."

Léontine reflected a moment, her pretty head on her hand.

" Do you know, dear Papa Bouchard," she said, after a while, " that you and I are engaged in what the Americans call a game of bluff ? "

" Don't know anything about the Americans. Don't know what bluff is."

" Oh, yes, you do — you know the thing, although you may not recognize the name. But you are a good soul, Papa Bouchard, and Victor and I *do* bother you a good deal; but only say no more of this matter — about Putzki and Louise — and don't tell Victor, and I 'll not tell Aunt Céleste, and everything will come perfectly right."

Papa Bouchard

As Léontine spoke she unclasped her necklace, kissed it, and with a gesture of scorn put on the real necklace, saying to herself: "I never thought I should come to this."

And then came a loud rat-tat at the door, and in walked Captain de Meneval again. He carried Monsieur Bouchard's impedimenta, with which he had so unceremoniously made off. Both he and Léontine looked thoroughly dis concerted at meeting each other. De Meneval thought she had gone away. Léontine blushed guiltily, and had barely enough presence of mind to cover up the necklace lying on the table with Papa Bouchard's scientific journal.

"Ah, good-evening, Papa Bouchard!" cried this arch hypocrite of an artillery captain, as if he had not seen Monsieur Bouchard half an hour before. "I came to return your umbrella and coat. Thanks very much for lending them to me in an emergency. Why, little girl,

Papa Bouchard

I thought you were on your way to the opera?"

"I am just going," answered Léontine, moving toward the door.

"One moment!" cried Papa Bouchard, waving his arm authoritatively. These two scapegraces had used him for their own purposes that night, had made game of him, and had threatened to discover a mare's nest to Mademoiselle Bouchard and had got seven thousand francs out of him in cold cash. Now, however, he would take his revenge. "Wait," he said to Léontine, who returned reluctantly to her former place.

Monsieur Bouchard, assuming the attitude and tone with which he addressed a couple of criminals in the pursuit of his professional duties, then continued:

"This is a very auspicious opportunity for me to speak to you both, in each other's presence, with a view to your mutual reform. Observe the

word; I use it advisedly." He paused.
Léontine trembled with apprehension,
while de Meneval surreptitiously mopped
his brow. "You have both of you
been very extravagant — wasteful, I
may say. Nothing that I have yet
said has availed to stop the outgo
of money far beyond your reasonable
wants — so *I* think. Now, I have
come to the conclusion that in order
for you to economize you must give
up your apartment. You must leave
Paris."

Leave Paris!

De Meneval was not so stunned but
that he could get up rather a ghastly
laugh.

"Leave Paris! Ha, ha! That's
little enough to me, Papa Bouchard —
Léontine and ballistics are all I want
to make me happy anywhere — but
Léontine — oh, I know she won't
go!"

"Won't she, eh? Not to an inexpensive little cottage outside of Paris

Papa Bouchard

— within striking distance of Melun, so you may go back and forth — a *very* inexpensive cottage?"

"Well, if that's your game," cried de Meneval, savagely, "there are plenty of cottages to be had at Melun. Our veterinarian has just given up his cottage — three rooms and a dog kennel. That's cheap enough. Shall I take it to-morrow for Captain and Madame de Meneval?"

"You are trifling, Monsieur le Capitaine," coolly answered Papa Bouchard. "You understand perfectly well what I mean."

"But, Papa Bouchard," put in Léontine, faintly, "while *I* don't object to the cottage, it would be cruel to Victor to force him away from Paris. It is so dull, anyway, at Melun. The only recreation he has is when he comes to Paris. Poor, poor Victor!"

Léontine was almost weeping — de Meneval was swearing between his teeth. Papa Bouchard was waving his arm about serene in the consciousness of power.

"I did not say you are to leave Paris to-night, or even to-morrow; perhaps a week — possibly a month — may be given you. But you are both too fond of gaieties, of clothes, of suppers and other dissipated things, and there are too many jewellers' shops in Paris." This thrust caused both of the culprits to quake. "So you must go to some retired place and economize."

"I see," replied de Meneval, who was thoroughly exasperated. "Having yourself practically run away from a quiet and respectable locality to these gay quarters, with young ladies of the ballet on every hand —" de Meneval pointed angrily to the red-and-gold young ladies on the walls — "now you wish to send my poor little wife off to some hole of a village, where one may exist but not live. I don't speak of myself — *I* don't care. It's for her."

Papa Bouchard

"Very well," answered Papa Bouchard, maliciously. "You may make that hole of a village a paradise steeped in dreamlike splendor to Léontine by your devoted and lover-like attentions to her. You can live over your honeymoon. Won't you like that, Léontine?"

"Y—yes," replied Léontine, dolefully.

"Some pretty rural place — all birds and flowers, eh? And a little dog. Does n't the prospect charm you?"

"Yes — only — for Victor ——"

"Have n't you just heard Victor say that all he needs to be perfectly happy are you and ballistics? So I suppose, Monsieur de Meneval, you will be revelling in rapture."

"I suppose so," replied de Meneval, gloomily. "Come, Léontine, shall I put you in the carriage? You won't have many chances of going to the opera, poor child, after this."

Léontine rose and said, coldly,

Papa Bouchard

"Good-night, Papa Bouchard." There was no tweaking of his ear, no patting of his bald head this time. They went

out like two sulky and disappointed children.

Papa Bouchard remained chuckling to himself. He had those two naughty young creatures in the hollow of his hand — it would be a good while before they would dare to be saucy to him —

and that little cottage in the suburbs was a fine idea. Strange it had not occurred to him before.

He seated himself in his easychair and began to review the events of his first day of liberty. His mind went back to the point where he had been interrupted by de Meneval's entrance — the point where the dear little bashful widow had appeared in his mind's eye. If he had been in the Rue Clarisse he would never even have dared to think of Madame Vernet, for his sister could actually read his thoughts. But here, in this jolly bachelor place, he could think about widows all he liked. And shutting his eyes the better to recall that slim, shrinking, gray-gowned figure, he opened them to see Madame Vernet quietly walking into the room, without knocking and quite as if she belonged there. She advanced to the table on one side of the room, laid her lace parasol on it and proceeded to remove her long gloves, but stopped in the midst of the process to rearrange a chair and to set straight a picture — one of Monsieur Bouchard's.

" This is very comfortable," she said, musingly, " but I can improve it — when I am settled here."

Papa Bouchard listened as if in a dream. He had not progressed so far as that. And then Madame Vernet, turning and seeing him, uttered a faint shriek, as if she had seen a snake instead of a human being, and ran — but not toward the door.

" My dear Madame Vernet, pray do not be alarmed. It is only I — Monsieur Bouchard," cried Papa Bouchard, striving to reassure her.

" Oh! is it you? Forgive me for being so agitated, but I am *so* easily frightened!" panted Madame Vernet. " Men always frighten me — I am the most timid woman in the world!"

" So I see," tenderly replied Papa Bouchard. He was standing quite close to Madame Vernet now, and she had clasped his arm and looked nervously about her, as if she expected another man to spring out of the fireplace or down from the ceiling.

"But when I saw it was only you, all my fears vanished," she continued. "And will you tell me to what I am indebted for the honor and pleasure of this visit ? "

"A question I was just asking myself. This is my new apartment."

"I beg pardon," replied Madame Vernet, "but it is *my* new apartment. I only moved into it to-day."

"And, Madame, I only moved into it to-day."

"It is number nine, fourth floor."

"No, Madame, it is number five, third floor."

"Ah," cried Madame Vernet. "I see. My apartment is directly over this, and corresponds with it exactly. I did not go up high enough, and I am not quite familiar with the surroundings. How absurd ! " and she laughed,

Papa Bouchard

showing the prettiest teeth in the world.

"How delightful!" replied Monsieur Bouchard, gallantly.

"And how singular! This is the third time in three days we have met by accident."

An uncomfortable recollection of Léontine's speech about accidents of this sort occurring in cycles flashed through Monsieur Bouchard's brain, but he dismissed the thought with energy. He rather relished accidents that brought about meetings with a woman as winning, as charming, as elegant as Madame Vernet; and then there was that deliciously intoxicating feeling of independence — no need to cut the interview short, no labored explanation to give Mademoiselle Céleste. Monsieur Bouchard was his own man now — for the first time, at fifty-four years of age. So he smiled benevolently, and said :

"I wish I might ask you to sit

95

down, but at least you will grant me permission to call on you."

"With pleasure," replied Madame Vernet. "And since you won't let me sit down — which, of course, would n't be proper, and I would n't commit the smallest impropriety for a million francs — at least let me walk about and look at your charming furnishings."

Papa Bouchard made a heartfelt apology for the red-and-gold young ladies on the walls who evidently shocked Madame Vernet extremely. He said he meant to take them down the next day. Madame Vernet replied with gentle severity that he ought to take them down that night. However, she went into raptures over " Kittens at Play " and " Socrates and His Pupils," which gave Papa Bouchard a high idea of her intellectuality.

But in the midst of a learned dissertation on " The Coliseum by Moonlight," Madame Vernet's eyes fell on the glittering paste necklace, which

Papa Bouchard

Monsieur Bouchard had left lying on the table. She picked it up gently — she did everything gently — and playfully clasping it round her neck, cried,

" How charming ! I won't ask you for whom this is intended ; for a sister, — a niece, perhaps. Lucky girl !"

" Indeed, it is not intended for any one," replied Monsieur Bouchard. " It is of trifling value — paste, at seventy-five francs to buy, and would sell for nothing."

" Nevertheless, it is very pretty," said Madame Vernet, looking at herself coquettishly in the mirror. And then, apparently forgetting all about the necklace, she confided to Monsieur Bouchard that she was so nervous at living alone — the only thing that reconciled her was that she had an uncle and an aunt living in the neighborhood who would watch over her. Monsieur Bouchard tried to reassure her, but Madame Vernet declined to be reassured. Her timidity was constitutional — she should

never be courageous as other women,
and so protesting, she gathered up her
parasol and gloves, and with blushing
apologies for her intrusion and a bash-

ful invitation to Monsieur Bouchard to
return her unique visit, made for the
door.

Monsieur Bouchard was charmed,
flattered, tickled and flustered beyond

expression, but he was likewise terrified at the thought that Madame Vernet had evidently forgotten that she had the necklace clasped round her throat and was going off with it. Paste though it was, Monsieur Bouchard had no mind to let it go out of his own hands. He followed her to the door, saying, " Madame, you have probably forgotten —— "

" Oh, no, I have n't," smilingly replied Madame Vernet ; " I know my own apartment now — it is number nine."

" But — but — you have inadvertently — er — a — " Poor Monsieur Bouchard mopped his forehead in his agony.

" Yes, quite inadvertently entered your apartment. Oh, how alarmed I was when I first saw you ! But you were so kind. Forgive me, and don't forget your promise to call. Good-bye."

And just as Monsieur Bouchard had

made up his mind to ask for the necklace she flitted out of the door.

Monsieur Bouchard sank, or rather
fell, into a chair. His head was in a
whirl. He felt as if the
events of that day were
beginning to be a little
too much for him. Just
at that moment Pierre ap-
peared from no one could
exactly say where.

"Come, now," said that
functionary, in a tone of
what Monsieur Bouchard
would have thought brazen familiarity
the day before, "I know all about it,
I saw the whole transaction; remember, Monsieur, we are pals now. She
can't get money on it any more than
Madame de Meneval can, and she'll
be sure to turn up again. Oh, you'll
come out all right, Monsieur. Cheer
up. We'll live a merry life, and
after all, it is something to be away
from that dreary old hole in the

Papa Bouchard

Rue Clarisse. Just listen, if you please."

Pierre ran to the window, threw it wide open, and the strains of rag time music from the music halls filled the room.

" Everything goes in rag time at this jolly place," cried Pierre — and then that staid, sober and decorous valet of thirty years' service, cut the pigeon wing, twirled around on one leg, with the other stuck stiffly out like a ballet dancer's, and kissing his hand in the direction of Madame Vernet's apartment, cried, " Oh, we're a gay pair of boys ! We mean to see life ! And no peaching on each other ! " And with ineffable impudence, he winked a Monsieur Bouchard.

Chapter II

MONSIEUR BOUCHARD
waked next morning with a
delicious sense of youth and irrespon-
sibility. There was no one to demand
an account of him for anything. As
for Pierre, Monsieur Bouchard determined to treat his vagaries in a jocular
manner — it was simply the honest
fellow's way of showing joy at his
emancipation. And when Pierre appeared, to shave his master, both of
them wore a cheerful air. It was their
14th of July.

Pierre, at the same time he brought
the hot water, brought Monsieur Bouchard's letters. What a comfort to
read them without having to give an
explanation of every one to Made-

Papa Bouchard

moiselle Céleste! Monsieur Bouchard actually enjoyed receiving his tailor's bill for the half-year under those circumstances. As for Pierre, he went about whistling like a whole flock of blackbirds, and Monsieur Bouchard had not the heart or the inclination to stop him. The only fly in Monsieur Bouchard's ointment was the unpleasant reflection that Madame Vernet still had the paste necklace, but he felt sure that she had discovered her inadvertence of the night before, and would return the thing during the day.

"I suppose," said Pierre, who seemed to have quite taken the direction of Monsieur Bouchard's affairs, "that Monsieur will be looking after the bills of Captain and Madame de Meneval to-day."

"I certainly shall," replied Monsieur Bouchard.

"And, Monsieur, you will find it necessary to go out to the Pigeon House at Melun to settle up Monsieur

le Capitaine's account without Madame
finding it out ? "

" I suppose so," answered Monsieur
Bouchard. " It is a nuisance; I never
was at Melun in my life."

" But that's no reason why Monsieur never should go to Melun; and
I 've been told that the Pigeon House is
a very gay place, with excellent wine.
Suppose Monsieur makes an evening
of it out there ? "

" Pierre," said Monsieur Bouchard,
wheeling around on him, " are you
trying to get me into all sorts of indiscretions in order to report me to the
Rue Clarisse ? "

" Lord, no, sir ! " replied Pierre,
with much readiness. " I am going
to the Moulin Rouge myself to-night,
and I 'm sure if my wife knew it she
would take not only my hair, but my
scalp with it, off my head. The
Moulin Rouge is a harmless enough
place, but that 's what 's been the matter
with our bringing up, Monsieur — we

were n't allowed to go to harmless places even. For my part, I mean to have my fling, even if my wife *does* find it out, and disciplines me. But there's no reason for either one of us being found out if we 'll only agree to stand by each other."

This was very satisfactory; in fact, everything seemed to be coming Monsieur Bouchard's way except — the paste necklace. The thought of that, like the ghost at Lady Macbeth's tea party, would not down. Monsieur Bouchard waited and lingered and dallied over his breakfast, and yet no parcel came from Madame Vernet. He did not care to remain at home all day waiting for it; no doubt it would come. It occurred to him that the best plan was to take Pierre completely into his confidence. It was true the rascal knew something of what had happened the night before, but Monsieur Bouchard felt it necessary, in Pierre's new rôle of trusty henchman and prime min-

ister, to confide all the particulars to
him. However, this must be done
in a manner consistent with the rela-
tions of master and man. So, when
Pierre was handing him his coat, hat
and gloves, preparatory to going out,
Monsieur Bouchard remarked, quite
casually, as if Pierre knew nothing of
the happenings of the night before :

"By the way, I am expecting a little
parcel to be sent me by Madame Vernet, the lady on the next floor, a very
pretty little woman — a widow——"

"Trust Monsieur for finding out all
the pretty little widows between here
and the Rue Clarisse," replied Pierre,
with the impudent grin that had scarce
left his face since he established himself in the Rue Bassano.

Now, this remark was not only
grossly familiar but grotesquely untrue,
so Monsieur Bouchard frowned and
said, sternly :

"You forget yourself."

"And all the pretty little widows

106

will have an eye on Monsieur," replied this unabashed reprobate of a Pierre.

At this Monsieur Bouchard wished to frown, but could not. Instead, his mouth came open in a pleased grin.

" Well, well, that may or may not be true. At all events, last night Madame Vernet, by the merest accident, came into this apartment, mistaking it for her own." Monsieur Bouchard paused. It was rather a difficult story to tell.

" By accident, did you say, Monsieur ? "

" Altogether by accident. A paste necklace belonging to Madame de Meneval was lying on my table, and Madame Vernet inadvertently carried it off. She will no doubt return it this morning. Take care of it when it comes."

" I will, sir, if it comes. But Monsieur will pardon me if I say I don't expect it to come — that is, if I know anything about women."

"But you *don't* know anything about women," curtly replied Monsieur Bouchard. Pierre was getting quite beside himself.

"True, Monsieur. I have been married thirty years. That is enough to convince the toughest sceptic who ever lived that he does n't know anything about women. But, all the same, Madame Vernet is n't going to send that necklace back."

Monsieur Bouchard turned pale and took an agitated turn about the room.

"Did Monsieur buy the paste necklace for — for — Mademoiselle Bouchard?" asked Pierre.

"No, you idiot! Did n't I tell you it belongs to Madame de Meneval — no — to Captain de Meneval — oh, the devil!"

Such expletives as this had been strictly forbidden in the Rue Clarisse, and in spite of his annoyance Monsieur

Papa Bouchard

Bouchard felt a sense of pleasure in being able to call on the devil in a casual and informal manner.

"I understand, Monsieur," replied Pierre, with the wink that, like the grin, appeared to have become constitutional with him since his advent in the Rue Bassano. "The accidental Madame Vernet appears to have become accidentally possessed of a paste necklace that is not hers. Accidents will happen; but one accident that I am sure will not occur is the return of the necklace."

"Damnation!" roared Monsieur Bouchard. He felt a delicious relish in saying this profane word. It was the first time in his life he had ever used it.

"Very well, Monsieur. Damnation or no damnation, I will keep the necklace for you — if I get it."

Monsieur Bouchard dashed down the stairs faster than he had ever done in his life before. But on reaching the street and adopting a decorous pace, he thought, " Of course it's nonsense to suppose that she won't return it. The fact is, I have got to discipline that Pierre. He has altogether forgotten himself, and I shall have to teach him a few lessons."

Meanwhile, in the gay little apartment in the Avenue de l'Impératrice, where the de Meneval *ménage* was situated, the necklace had become a haunting ghost as well as in the Rue Bassano.

As Léontine and her husband sat opposite each other at breakfast in the pretty little *salle à manger*, each felt like a criminal. It was a very pretty little *salle à manger* — just the sort of room for a young couple with a modest income, yet sufficient to live on. But there is not a young couple in existence who, knowing that their income is cut exactly in half while the other half is saved up for them, would be satisfied with their moiety. This,

Papa Bouchard

however, was bliss compared to the
prospect of that dreary little cottage in
the country to which Papa Bouchard
had condemned them — or rather, to
which they had condemned each other

— for each thought secretly that but
for those unlucky debts and the diamond necklace, Papa Bouchard would
never have been so hard on them.
The most painful part of it was, however, the necessity of concealment each

felt toward the other. They had, up to this time, lived their married life with the perfect frankness of two devoted young persons who love and confide in each other — and this was what it had come to — bitterly thought de Meneval, who truly loved his pretty little wife — her diamonds practically put in pawn by him with that old curmudgeon, who had got thereby just the opportunity he wanted to exile them from Paris. All these thoughts chased through his mind as he looked at Léontine with a new and unpleasant conviction that he was a villain.

Léontine, for her part, felt a horrid heart-sickness when she remembered the paste necklace quietly reposing in the strong-box in her dressing-room, while Victor's wedding gift was in Papa Bouchard's strong-box in the Rue Bassano. And that dull little house in the country! It was she who had brought all this on Victor, and the thought filled her heart with remorseful tenderness toward her husband. She addressed him by the fondest names as she poured his coffee for him.

"And you have to go to that tiresome Melun to-day, to be away from me two whole days?"

"Yes," replied de Meneval. "How I wish you could go with me! I have often been sorry I gave up my quarters to accommodate Lefebvre, with his wife and four children to support on her *dot* and his captain's pay. I did n't mind living *en garçon* until I had a wife of my own."

It was quite true that de Meneval, out of generosity, had given up the best part of his quarters to his brother officer, and had not the heart to ask for them again, especially as he was generally supposed to be in the enjoyment of a large income.

"Don't say you are sorry, Victor. For my part, charming as it would be to stay at Melun with you, I am glad you can help the poor Lefebvres. *We* know what it is to want money, don't we ? "

" Indeed we do."

" And our case is the harder that no one will believe we have n't the use of our money."

Léontine, who was delicate-minded, always called her money " our money," and de Meneval deeply and affectionately appreciated this.

" And it will be duller than ever at that odious little cottage in the suburbs of Melun."

" Oh, yes. Léontine, I am afraid it is I who have brought this on you."

" No, no, no — it is I, or rather Papa Bouchard's old-fashioned, stingy ideas. He has no notion of what a modern way of living costs."

" But he will find out in the Rue Bassano, if I 'm not mistaken," said de Meneval, laughing suddenly.

Then there was a long pause, broken by Léontine's throwing down her napkin and crying out :

Papa Bouchard

"I have an inspiration! We are so dull and disheartened to-day that nothing but a supper at the Pigeon House will cheer us up. You will take me there to-night. Remember, you promised me."

"Did I?" asked poor de Meneval. He was, in truth, afraid to show his face at the Pigeon House lest the head waiter should quietly tap him on the shoulder and ask him to step up to the bureau and pay the whole of the nineteen hundred francs. And what would become of that story he had told Léontine about never having set foot in the Pigeon House since his marriage? Only the week before, there had been a little supper — de Meneval's recollection of it was rather cloudy — but he thought he remembered something about going to sleep on a bench, and waking up and finding an umbrella in his sword-belt instead of his sword. This scheme of Léontine's was most unlucky.

Papa Bouchard

"And I must and will go this very evening!" cried Léontine, jumping up and running around to her husband's chair, where she proceeded to perch herself on the arm. "I know exactly how it can be done. I will take the eight o'clock train. You will meet me at the station. We will go to the Pigeon House, where you will secure a table in that charming terrace garden you have told me so much about. We will have a jolly little supper — and I'll pay for the champagne. No — no!" putting her hands over de Meneval's mouth. "And it will be such fun to watch the queer people passing in and out of the music hall!"

"Some of them," said de Meneval, with the hope of frightening Léontine, "are very queer indeed."

"Yes, yes, I know. You have often told me about the singers and dancers coming out there in their theatre clothes, and that's just what I want to see. And as for any impropriety —

have n't I often heard you say that every one of those hard-working ballet girls is supporting her bedridden parents, or crippled husband, or something of the sort ? "

" I *did* say that many of them are honest and hard-working."

" I am sure of it ! The mere fact that they work is enough. You know I have been studying sociology of late, and I know something about the working people." Léontine, as she said this, had an uncomfortable twinge when she remembered Putzki and Louise.

Now, if anything in the world was calculated to make the bright June morning blacker than it was already to de Meneval, it was this sudden freak of Léontine's to go out to the Pigeon House to supper. He fidgeted in his chair, and hummed and ha'd, but Léontine prattled on, talking about the amusement she should have.

" And I shall at last meet Major

117

Fallière! I am so anxious to know him, the dear old thing!"

"Fallière won't be at Melun to-night. He goes to Châlons on special duty to-day," cried de Meneval, seeing a gleam of hope. "Why not wait until he comes back — some time next week?"

"Oh, it is quite useless waiting for an officer. He may be snatched up at any time and packed off to the ends of the earth. And go to the Pigeon House to-night I shall, I will, I must —" she punctuated this sentence by giving de Meneval three charming kisses — "and if it's very improper, so much the better! I shall go to the Rue Clarisse and tell Aunt Céleste you forced me to go against my will, and so escape a scolding."

"That's all very well," replied poor de Meneval, "but how will you get back to-night? I can't leave — and I don't know of anyone returning to Paris."

Papa Bouchard

" Don't bother your head about that.
You will put me on the train at Melun
— my maid will meet me at the St.
Lazare station. What could be simpler? No, no, no! I shall sup with
you to-night at the Pigeon House, so
be sure and meet me at the station at
half-past eight o'clock — you have just
time to make your train." And she
flew into his room, brought out his
helmet and sword — for he was in uniform, being ready to report for duty —
and kissing him affectionately, pushed
him out of the door. De Meneval ran
down the stairs and, jumping into a
cab, drove rapidly off. He waved his
hand to Léontine, watching him from
the balcony.

Deceits and concealments were a
new burden for Léontine to carry, and
she spent a wretched day. Do what
she would, she saw her diamond necklace at every turn. It haunted her as
the dagger haunted the Scotch lady in
the play. Still woebegone, she deter-

Papa Bouchard

mined to go to see Aunt Céleste in the
Rue Clarisse. What a dismal old
street it was, anyhow! Dark and dull
and utterly without life — no wonder
Papa Bouchard had tired of it and had
levanted into a gayer precinct. When
she was ushered into Mademoiselle
Bouchard's dingy little drawing-room
she found that good woman, Aunt
Céleste, seated with one eye on her
embroidery and the other on Élise,
who was polishing up the already shin-
ing furniture. Aunt Céleste's usually
placid face was troubled, but it lighted
up when she saw Léontine running in.
Aunt Céleste was genuinely fond of the
girl, albeit she was in chronic spasms
over Léontine's modern, and to poor
Mademoiselle Céleste's notion, outland-
ish ideas. Still, they really loved each
other, and kissed affectionately.

" Well, Aunt Céleste, how do you
stand Papa Bouchard's absence ? " asked
Léontine, jokingly, but not unkindly.

Mademoiselle Bouchard wagged her

head disconsolately. "It is not how I stand it. It is how he, poor, dear boy, stands it. Who will look after his dinner and see that he has simple

and wholesome food? Who will look to his flannels? Who will see that he lays aside his books at ten o'clock and goes to bed, as he has always been accustomed?"

Papa Bouchard

"It seems to me, Aunt Céleste, that as Papa Bouchard is fifty-four years of age he ought to know something about taking care of himself."

"But he does n't. However, I have given him Pierre. I have the greatest confidence in Pierre. In thirty years I have never known him to be guilty of an indiscretion. He was very unwilling to go, poor fellow. He is truly attached to the quiet and decorum of the Rue Clarisse, and objected very much to the noise and bustle of the Rue Bassano, with so many theatres about and people turning night into day. I almost had to force him to go — but I did it on my poor, dear brother's account. Pierre is to come to see me every day to tell me just how the dear boy has passed his time."

Léontine sincerely hoped that Pierre would not think it necessary to mention her visit to Papa Bouchard the night before.

"And I have had another sorrow,"

continued poor Mademoiselle Bouchard. "My parrot — Pierrot — that I have had for seventeen years, and taught so many moral and useful aphorisms — he, too, has deserted me."

"All three of them vanished — like this — *pouf !* " Élise put in, with the freedom of an old servant. "Monsieur Bouchard, that good-for-nothing husband of mine and Pierrot — and all bent on mischief — that I 'll swear to ! "

Mademoiselle Bouchard proceeded to read Élise a lecture on the duties of the married state, among the first of which was the obligation of the wife to believe everything her husband tells her, at which Élise laughed grimly.

"Mademoiselle is joking, ha, ha ! "

Although Mademoiselle Bouchard led so retired a life, she liked well enough to know what was going on in the outside world, if only to be shocked at it. So, when Léontine told her about the proposed supper at the Pigeon House that evening, Mademoiselle Bouchard was duly horrified, terrified and mortified, but she did not forget to charge Léontine to come and tell her all the dreadful things she saw at that unconventional place.

Léontine, after spending the morning in the Rue Clarisse, returned to her own apartment in the Avenue de l'Impératrice. She was so dispirited at the contemplation of her own faults and Victor's supposed Spartan virtue that she had no heart to take her usual afternoon automobile excursion in the Bois de Boulogne — the automobile being one of the few indulgences she had been able to screw out of Papa Bouchard. She remained at home, therefore, until it was time to take the eight o'clock train for Melun. Then, taking her maid to the St. Lazare station, and directing her to be there when the eleven o'clock train from Melun returned, Léontine stepped into a first-class compartment, and was soon speeding toward Melun.

Papa Bouchard

She wore a beautiful evening costume concealed by a long silk cloak,
and a charming hat was perched on
her dainty head. The thought in her
tender little heart was of the pleasure
her society would give her dear Victor.

But her dear Victor had spent the
day in a manner not unlike her own.
He had interviewed the proprietor of
the Pigeon House and had paid half the
bill. The transaction had involved
the mortifying admission that before the
balance was handed over Monsieur
Bouchard would be out there himself
to look into the matter, as if Captain
de Meneval were a naughty schoolboy.
The proprietor of the Pigeon House
had scoffed heartlessly at this, and de
Meneval had difficulty in keeping from
knocking him down for his impudence.
Then — Léontine's visit ! What impish microbe had lodged in her head,
inducing her to come out there ? He
knew her to be keen of wit, and it would
be difficult to disguise from her his

Papa Bouchard

familiarity with the place. He might, it is true, say he knew little or nothing about it, but the waiters, especially one François, who knew his taste in wines and cigars, fish and *entrées* and *hors d'œuvres* to a dot, would be sure to betray him. And then, the diamond necklace lay heavy on his heart and danced up and down before his eyes, for Victor de Meneval really loved his charming young wife, and argued to himself that if that stingy old hunks of a Papa Bouchard had not held him so tight the present predicament would not have existed.

However, time waits for no man; and when the eight o'clock train from Paris was due Captain de Meneval was at the little station waiting for it. And when it rolled in Léontine sprang gracefully out of her compartment.

As in the morning, each felt remorseful and penitent toward the other and tried to make up for the wrong that each had secretly done the other by

renewed demonstrations of affection.
When de Meneval escorted his charming wife across the street to the Pigeon
House, which was only a step away, he
paid her the prettiest and most loverlike
compliments imaginable. Léontine responded with the sweetest smiles and
the tenderest words; so that by the
time they reached the terrace garden
through a covered hedge next the
Pigeon House itself, each felt like a
thief and a murderer.

Léontine exclaimed with delight at
the beauty of the terrace garden. It
was indeed a pretty and cheerful place.
It looked down straight into a little
valley where the river meandered. An
iron railing and a stone coping defined
the terrace. Trees and shrubbery,
pretty flower beds and a rustic arbor
were lighted by incandescent lamps that
gleamed softly in the purple glow of
evening. The windows of the Pigeon
House gave directly on the terrace,
and already the glittering lights and the

sounds of the orchestra showed that the performance was beginning. There were only a few persons scattered about, and the waiters were collected in groups, whispering, while waiting for customers. One, however — the identical François, whom de Meneval wished to avoid — ran forward and showed them a pleasant table. He was in the act of saying, "What will Monsieur le Capitaine have?" when de Meneval, looking him straight in the face, though addressing Léontine, said :

"It's been so long since I've seen this place — not since our marriage, in fact — that I hardly know what it is like."

"Oho!" thought François, "that is your game, is it? Very well, Monsieur, I will help you out with it — for a consideration." Then, extending his hand for de Meneval's hat, he gave a slight but significant twitch of his fingers and palm, to which a ten-franc piece was the agreeable response. "Since Monsieur is evidently not familiar with this place," said the wily François, " perhaps he will allow me to recommend our white soup, to begin with."

" Thank you," replied de Meneval; " and can you also recommend this turbot on the menu ? "

" Yes, Monsieur. If you had ever tasted our turbot you would never look at turbot outside of the Pigeon House."

" By the way, what is your name ? "

" François, if you please."

François remembered perfectly, that little supper at the Pigeon House the week before, when Captain de Meneval had not only forgotten François's name but his own as well, and so had several other very jolly officers. But François, though but a waiter, had the soul of a gentleman, and was nobly oblivious of ever having set eyes on Captain de Meneval before.

Papa Bouchard

"Now, Victor," said Léontine, who had been studying the wine list, "as I invited myself here to-night, I intend to be part host. I claim the right of providing the wine and cigars. They shall be of the best, as the best of husbands deserves." Then, turning to François, she said: "Your best Chambertin with the soup, and a bottle of this 1840 Bordeaux, and a bottle of Veuve Clicquot. Also, for Monsieur le Capitaine some of your Reina Regente cigars." Léontine returned to her study of the wine list and de Meneval and François exchanged sympathetic grins. François vanished after having received a very expensive order.

Left to themselves, Léontine and Victor began to condole with each other on the prospect of their rustication.

"It is not for myself I grieve," declared Léontine, "it is for you, poor darling."

"Never mind me," protested de

Papa Bouchard

Meneval. "If only *you* were not condemned to that infernal little cottage!
Well, we shall have one good dinner,
anyhow, before we begin doing time,
as it were."

And as they were exchanging their
lugubrious confidences, a shriek of
hoarse laughter resounded near them,
and there on the arbor hung a cage
with a parrot in it which Léontine immediately recognized as Pierrot. With

gurgles of laughter Léontine told Victor of her visit to the Rue Clarisse that morning and the flight of Pierrot, along with that of Papa Bouchard and Pierre.

" And I shall go to-morrow morning and tell Aunt Céleste that I have seen her dear Pierrot."

" It will be cruelty to animals to take the poor devil back to the Rue Clarisse," replied de Meneval.

François then returned with the soup and fish, both of which were excellent. De Meneval made a point of calling François " Louis " or " Adolphe " occasionally, and François never failed to respectfully correct him.

Meanwhile, sweet sounds of the orchestra and of singing floated out from the open windows of the Pigeon House. More people strolled on the terrace, including many officers of the garrison; and when the intermission came, a flock of girls, each escorted by a young man, generally an officer, came out, laughing and chattering, and took their places at the little tables. Some had only a glass of lemonade or wine,

others had time for a pâté or some trifle of the kind. It was very pretty and picturesque, and Léontine, never having seen anything of the kind, was delighted.

De Meneval was in agony lest some

133

Papa Bouchard

of his friends among the ladies should recognize him, but they, being mostly decent and self-respecting women, though of a humble class, with true French politeness did not intrude themselves on his notice in any way. Nor was he anxious to begin a conversation with any of his brother officers, and carefully avoided noticing them beyond a bow, although many of them would have been glad of an introduction to his pretty young wife.

The dinner was outwardly very jolly, but the demon of remorse was at work within the breasts of both Victor and Léontine. Nevertheless, it did not affect their appetites, and François found he had a good deal to do. At last, however, coffee was served, and just as Léontine put down her cup a scream from the parrot resounded.

" Ah, there you are, Papa Bouchard! Up to mischief, eh, Papa Bouchard! Bad boy Bouchard ! "

Now these were some of the phrases

134

Papa Bouchard

that Léontine herself, during her so-
journ in the Rue Clarisse, had taught
the parrot, much to her own and Papa
Bouchard's amusement. The wicked
bird remembered them most inopper-
tunely, for there was Papa Bouchard
himself strolling into the
garden.

"Good heavens!" cried
de Meneval. "We can't
afford to let Papa Bouchard
see us out here. We should
be sent into retirement to-
morrow morning!" And
obeying a mutual impulse,
these two graceless creatures
flew round the corner of the
arbor, where they could see
without being seen.

Monsieur Bouchard entered with an
air of affected jauntiness which went
very well with the extreme youthful-
ness of his attire. Apparently he had
thrown all his old clothes to the winds,
along with his discretion, when he

135

Papa Bouchard

decamped from the Rue Clarisse. He
wore an extremely youthful suit of
light gray, with a flaming necktie, a
collar that nearly cut his ears off, and a
watch chain that would have answered
either for a watch or a dog. A huge
red rose decorated his lapel, and his
scanty hair, when he removed his hat,
showed marks of the curling-iron.

At the first shriek from the parrot
Papa Bouchard started apprehensively.
The waiters — a shrewd and vexatious
lot, who never fail to notice all the
slips of elderly gentlemen — immediately jumped to the right conclusion,
that the elderly gentleman in youthful
attire was an old acquaintance of the
newly acquired parrot. Monsieur Bouchard felt, rather than saw, a simultaneous snicker go round, and rightly
concluding that the best thing to do
was to ignore the wicked Pierrot,
walked away from the arbor, and seating himself at a table some distance
away, pulled out of his pocket the *Jour-*

Papa Bouchard

nal des Débats and read it diligently.
The parrot, however, delighted to find
an old acquaintance among so many
new faces, continued to call out, at
intervals, various remarks to Papa Bouchard, such as " Does the old lady
know you 're out ? " " Oh, you are a
gay bird, Papa Bouchard ! " and always
winding up, like a Greek chorus, with
" Bad boy Bouchard ! "

Presently a waiter approached and
asked Monsieur Bouchard politely what
he wished to be served with, and before
he could ask for his usual drink, a little
sugared water, the diabolical Pierrot
screeched out, " An American cock-
tail ! " which the bird pronounced
" cockee-tailee." Papa Bouchard
scowled. This was very annoying.

" A little sugared water, if you
please," he replied to the waiter, and
the bird, on hearing it, burst into a
screech of hoarse laughter.

Monsieur Bouchard laid down his
newspaper and looked about him with

curiosity not unmixed with gratifica-
tion. Everything seemed extremely
jolly — these places were undoubtedly

pleasant, and he was not so much surprised as he had been at de Meneval's
fondness for it. At that very moment
de Meneval and Léontine were watch-

ing him and counting the chances of slipping out without being caught. But Papa Bouchard, quite unconscious of this, was becoming more and more interested in what was going on before him and around him. "At these places, though," he was thinking, "one should have a companion — a person of the other sex — someone to help one enjoy — it's dreary trying to be happy alone." And as if in answer to his thought, he saw, entering the garden in both haste and embarrassment, the charming Madame Vernet.

Now, a curious thing happened — a psychologic mystery. All day long Monsieur Bouchard had been haunted and troubled by the thought of Madame Vernet and the paste necklace. She had not returned it. So much he knew from his first look at Pierre's countenance when he had got home that afternoon. But the minute he saw the lady herself, in his pleased flutter and twitter of enjoyment, the necklace vanished from his consciousness; he remembered only that she was pretty, she was young, she was demure and she was easily alarmed. In fact, Madame Vernet appeared to be scared half to death at this very instant, and as soon as she caught sight of Monsieur Bouchard she fled toward him like a frightened bird.

"Oh, Monsieur Bouchard!" she said, panting and agitated, "how relieved I am to find you here! I had an appointment to meet my uncle and aunt here — you remember I told you I had an uncle and aunt living at Melun whom I often visited — and not seeing them outside I took it for granted they were inside, and so came in. I felt terribly embarrassed — I am so diffident, you know — at entering such a place alone, but I expected every moment to see them, and when I did not I thought I should have fainted from sheer terror — you can't imagine what a timid little thing I am — and

140

then my eyes fell on you, and I said to myself: 'There is that dear, good, handsome Monsieur Bouchard — he is the very man to take care of a poor, terrified woman' — and so I ran to you." Madame Vernet dropped on a chair at Monsieur Bouchard's table.

What man with a soul as big as the head of a pin could refuse succor to a pretty woman under these circumstances! Not Papa Bouchard.

"My dear Madame Vernet," he said, "pray compose yourself. I will take care of you until your uncle and aunt arrive."

Madame Vernet looked around apprehensively.

"I don't see my uncle and aunt," she murmured — which was perfectly true — "and I am afraid, very much afraid, Monsieur Bouchard, that your youthful appearance really unfits you for the office of chaperon."

Oh, how happy was Papa Bouchard at that! With liberty seemed to have come youth — with youth should come champagne. Papa Bouchard called the waiter back and changed his order from a glass of sugared water to a quart of extra dry Veuve Clicquot.

" Now," said he, playfully taking up Madame Vernet's fan, " don't worry your little head about your uncle and aunt. I'll be your uncle and aunt for this evening. I'm sure I have been told by a number of persons — members of my own family — that the Pigeon House is a perfectly respectable place. So let us have a pleasant evening here, and I will take you back to Paris by the eleven o'clock train."

" Oh, Monsieur Bouchard, there is nothing I should like better, but I am afraid —— "

" Don't, don't be afraid. There is n't the least chance of anyone I know turning up. I have a young jackanapes of a family connection stationed here — a young officer — but I think I have pretty effectually shut

142

the door of the Pigeon House in *his* face."

At that very moment this young jackanapes of an officer was watching and listening to Papa Bouchard with the most entrancing delight. So was Léontine, who could not refrain from pinching de Meneval in her ecstasy. The enjoyment of these two young scapegraces was enhanced at this very moment by the parrot screaming out:

"Oh, naughty old Bouchard! I 'll tell the old lady! Bad boy Bouchard!"

Madame Vernet started and looked inquiringly at the bird. Papa Bouchard was seriously vexed.

"Pray," he said, in an annoyed voice, "don't pay any attention to that ridiculous bird. I always thought parrots were the incarnation of the devil. I can't imagine how the creature found out my name. At all events," he added, tenderly, "neither bird nor devil, neither man nor woman, nor even your

143

aunt and uncle, can spoil the evening for us."

" I don't think my aunt and uncle can be coming," replied Madame Vernet. And she spoke the truth.

"So much the better," whispered Papa Bouchard.

The waiter, the same astute François who had waited on de Meneval and Léontine, now appeared with the champagne. Monsieur Bouchard had not thought of ordering anything to eat, but when this artful François said to him, " Did Monsieur ask for a menu card ? " Monsieur Bouchard replied, promptly, " Certainly I did."

The menu was brought, and Monsieur Bouchard, with his head close to Madame Vernet's, studied it attentively. His order as finally made out would have caused an earthquake in the Rue Clarisse. He ordered everything that had been strictly forbidden during the last thirty years. The order bore, too, a really remarkable resem-

Papa Bouchard

blance to the one given by the de Menevals, except that those happy-go-lucky young people had not the money to pay for it, and Monsieur Bouchard had.

Never in all his life had Papa Bouchard enjoyed a supper as much as that one. He was at perfect liberty to eat and drink all the things that were certain to make him feel ill the next day, a prerogative dear to a man's heart. He had a charming woman opposite him, and a waiter who fairly overwhelmed him with attentions. Without an order from Monsieur Bouchard, François produced the wine appropriate to every course, and instead of being frowned on was rewarded for it. But in spite of white wines and red wines, Papa Bouchard stuck pretty close to the champagne, which speedily got into his tongue and his eyes as well as into his blood. It was the champagne that made him squeeze Madame Vernet's hand under the table, wink at François

10   145

Papa Bouchard

and kiss his fingers to one of the young
ladies of the ballet, who responded by
playfully throwing a bouquet to him

which hit him on the nose. In fact,
his enjoyment would have been entirely
without alloy but for Pierrot, who,
slyly inspired by the waiters, kept up a

running fire of remarks, always ending
in a shrill laugh and a yell of "Bad
boy Bouchard!"

If Pierrot bothered Papa Bouchard
slightly, he added immensely to the
suppressed gaiety of the two listeners,
de Meneval and Léontine, and they
went off into spasms of silent laughter
whenever Pierrot screamed out any
appropriate remark.

Papa Bouchard, however, got a good
deal of solid enjoyment out of his
supper in spite of his old friend of the
Rue Clarisse, and Pierrot did not inter-
fere in the least with Madame Vernet's
pleasure.

"The fact is," said Monsieur Bouchard, confidentially, to Madame Vernet, after the third glass of champagne,
"I was n't quite candid about that
devilish bird." Papa Bouchard used
this wicked word with the greatest
relish. "It belonged to my sister —
older than I — who brought me up
in the way I should go, and a deuced

dull and uncomfortable way it was!
A day or two ago, Pierrot — that's the
parrot's name — got tired of the propriety and seclusion of the Rue Clarisse, where we have lived for thirty
years, just as Pierre, my man-servant,
did, and I myself. All at once, without any previous consultation, Pierre,
Pierrot and I levanted, so to speak.
Pierrot has evidently got caught —
which is more than I intend to be —
but I'm sure he finds the Pigeon House
a great improvement on the Rue Clarisse,
and I have n't the heart to return him
there. You don't know how pleasant
it is to be living in the Rue Bassano
after thirty years in the Rue Clarisse.
And to be my own man, instead of
my sister's — excellent woman she is,
excellent, but she does n't understand
what a young man of the present day
— er — I mean a man with the feelings
of youth, requires to make him happy.
So that 's why I eloped."

"It 's a great mistake not to give

Papa Bouchard

a man his head sometimes," added Madame Vernet, with one of her gentle and winning smiles.

"Yes, yes, yes. You know how to manage a man, I see."

"*I* manage a man!" cried Madame Vernet. "Pray don't say that. The idea of my managing a great, strong man! No, indeed! All I should ask of a man is that he would manage me — and I'm sure, as yielding as I am, nothing would be easier."

At which François, behind Monsieur Bouchard's chair, doubled up with laughter, and Léontine had to fan de Meneval, who appeared to be choking in an agony of enjoyment, while Pierrot varied his performance by beginning to sing the song from the opera, "Ah, I have sighed to rest me!"

"Well," continued Papa Bouchard, whose *bonhomie* increased with every sip of champagne, "I suppose I shall have to manage a woman some day, for, to be very confidential, my dear

Papa Bouchard

Madame Vernet, I am in an excellent position to marry, and after a while I think I shall not be satisfied with liberty. I shall want power, too — the power of controlling another destiny, another heart, another will besides my own; so I shall marry a wife." Papa Bouchard said this with an air of the greatest determination, swelling out his waistcoat, and at the same moment the parrot shrieked out laughing, " Oh, what an old fool ! "

" What 's that ? What 's that ? " cried Monsieur Bouchard, indignantly, turning to François. He was a little confused by the champagne and Madame Vernet's bright eyes.

" If you please, Monsieur, it is that troublesome parrot. I shall tell the proprietor how very annoying the bird is — he has only just got it — and I am sure to-morrow morning it will be sent away."

Monsieur Bouchard had to be satisfied with this. His enjoyment, how-

Papa Bouchard

ever, was now too deep for Pierrot to ruffle except for a moment. Monsieur Bouchard was living — living cycles of time, and life was taking on a color, an exuberance, a melody that quite turned his otherwise excellent head. He was delighted with Madame Vernet's exposition of her inability and indisposition to manage a man. "That 's the sort of wife I 'll have when I marry," he thought to himself, taking another shy at the champagne. "None of your managing sort — I 've been managed too much already, heaven knows." And inspired by these pleasing reflections, he said, tenderly, to Madame Vernet, offering her his arm:

"Come, Madame, let us take a little stroll in search of your uncle and aunt. Do you see that sweet, retired little alley, all roses and myrtles and honeysuckles, with a lot of cooing pigeons nestling among them? Perhaps we may find your uncle and aunt

amid the roses. And, Madame, I may
say to you, I don't want a managing
wife, and I don't know any man who
does. I want a dependent creature —
sturdy oak and clinging vine, you know
— I want a clinger. And if she has
already tried her hand on another man,
so much the better. I get the benefit
of her experience. The fact is, Madame, I was born to console — I 'm a
consoler of the first water. Now, pray
take my arm and let us explore the
wilderness of roses and myrtles."

Madame Vernet hung her head, but
Papa Bouchard insisted. When at last
she rose she threw aside the graceful
little wrap round her shoulders, and
there, gleaming on her throat, was the
paste necklace.

Monsieur Bouchard received a distinct and unpleasant shock as he recognized the troublesome object, and
he was nowise relieved by Madame
Vernet saying, in her softest and most
insinuating manner:

Papa Bouchard

" How charming it was of you to give me this lovely ornament ! "

Monsieur Bouchard would have dropped Madame Vernet's arm, but she held on to him. This was certainly a very disagreeable incident. He had not given her the necklace — he never dreamed of giving it to her — he had been very much annoyed at her failure to return it, and ——

But what were Monsieur Bouchard's feelings in comparison with those of Léontine and de Meneval, both of whom were watching every movement of Papa Bouchard and Madame Vernet ? Their laughing faces changed like magic. They stood — Léontine and Victor — horror-stricken, and as if turned to stone, each pale, trembling, and afraid to meet the eye of the other. But as, after a minute or two of agonized surprise, they began to recover from the first shock of their discovery, they felt the necessity of concealing their feelings from each other, and at the same time not losing sight of the forty thousand franc necklace.

Léontine, womanlike, was the first to rally. She was quite pale — de Meneval was not sure whether she had recognized the necklace or not, and he was afraid to ask. Her voice trembled slightly as she said :

"I think I'll go and speak to Papa Bouchard. It will be such — such fun to let him know we have been watching him all the time."

Out of sheer stupidity, and being thoroughly disconcerted, de Meneval walked along with her toward Monsieur Bouchard and Madame Vernet. Léontine jumped to the conclusion that he suspected something. So she stopped short and said, in a voice that she vainly tried to make laughing and merry :

"Let me have Papa Bouchard to myself — it will be the more amusing if you appear later on."

"Certainly," replied de Meneval,

Papa Bouchard

and continued to walk with her
toward Papa Bouchard and Madame
Vernet. The fact is, he had not
heard a word of what Léontine was
saying. Papa Bouchard was standing
in front of Madame Vernet, and his
countenance showed that all was not
at ease within. She had asked him
to button her glove, and he could not
well refuse, but the sight of the necklace was rather trying to his nerves.
And in the midst of it appeared the
two human beings he least desired
to see on earth — Léontine and de
Meneval!

The three stood looking at each
other like a trio of criminals. Madame
Vernet, the blushing, the bashful, the
diffident, was the only one of the
four who was not cruelly embarrassed.
And then, besides the infernal necklace — for so Papa Bouchard char-
acterized it in his new vocabulary —
the idea of being caught supping with
a lady at the Pigeon House! Suppose

those two scamps should fly off to the
Rue Clarisse with the gruesome tale
— and he did n't know exactly how
much champagne he had taken, only
his head was buzzing a little — poor,
poor Papa Bouchard! However, it
would never do to show the white
feather in the beginning; the champagne had given him some Dutch
courage, but it did not supply him
with any judgment, for his first remark
was about the most indiscreet he could
have made. Assuming, or trying to
assume, his usual authoritative air, he
said to de Meneval:

" Monsieur le Capitaine, I thought
there was a distinct understanding between us that there were to be no more
suppers at the Pigeon House. And
bringing your wife to this place ——— "

" I know of no such understanding,
Monsieur Bouchard," replied de Meneval, with some spirit. " I deny your
right, or that of any other man, to
say where I shall have supper with my

Papa Bouchard

wife. If the Pigeon House is proper
enough for you and this lady — " de
Meneval indicated Madame Vernet,
who, with her usual bashfulness, had
retired a little — " whom I overheard
just now thanking you for the superb
necklace she wears, it is assuredly proper
for me and for my wife."

This was unanswerable logic, and
Papa Bouchard was momentarily staggered by it. De Meneval followed up
his advantage by saying, significantly,
" To-morrow morning I shall come to
see you, and you will kindly explain
to me some mysteries concerning — "
De Meneval stopped short; he could
not speak his mind to Monsieur Bouchard without letting the terrible and
menacing cat out of the bag regarding
the necklace.

It was now Léontine's turn at the
poor gentleman.

" Come, Papa Bouchard," she said,
with pallid lips, but affecting to laugh,
" you must not scold Victor for bring-

ing me here. I really made him do it.
But I want to speak to you a moment
in that sweet, sequestered arbor, where
you told this lady just now she might

find her uncle and aunt, amid the roses
and honeysuckles and the little cooing
pigeons."

Monsieur Bouchard would much
rather have gone off with a gendarme

at that very moment, but Léontine
had him by the arm, and was determinedly dragging him away. An
anxious grin appeared on his countenance as he turned to Madame Vernet
and said :

" One moment, Madame, and I will
return."

" Only a moment, remember," answered this bashful creature.

Madame Vernet had not the slightest objection to being left in charge
of this good-looking young officer.
She cast down her eyes and began to
murmur something about her timidity,
when she was brought up all standing
by de Meneval saying :

" Madame, a few moments ago I
overheard you thanking Monsieur
Bouchard for that superb necklace you
wear."

Madame Vernet smiled. Superb
necklace, indeed ! It must be a fine
imitation.

" But," continued de Meneval,

"that necklace belongs to my wife, Madame de Meneval. I myself selected it, and paid forty thousand francs for it. Last night I left it in Monsieur Bouchard's care in the Rue Bassano. To-night I find you, a woman with whom, I am sure, Monsieur Bouchard has a very casual acquaintance, wearing my wife's forty thousand franc necklace. You will admit that the circumstances justify me in demanding the necklace."

" Monsieur," replied Madame Vernet, " this necklace is paste. It cost only seventy-five francs. I have Monsieur Bouchard's word for it."

" The old sinner! Well, Monsieur Bouchard was n't saying his prayers when he told you that. I tell you the stones are real, and unless you hand the necklace over to me this instant I shall telephone for a couple of policemen — there is a police station not two minutes away — and to-morrow morning you and Monsieur Bouchard can explain the matter in the police court."

Now, Madame Vernet was really as brave as a lion. She suspected at once that she had got hold of something of actual value, and she determined to hold on to it and get away with it ; hence nothing could have been more pleasing to her at that moment than to have de Meneval out of the way for a few moments — even to fetch a policeman — so she merely replied, with calm assurance :

" Do as you like, Monsieur. I never saw you before — I hope I shall never see you again. My protector is at hand, and when you arrive with your police officers it is Monsieur Bouchard with whom you will have to settle."

De Meneval turned and ran out of the garden toward the police station. He thought that exposure was coming anyhow, and he had better secure the stakes in the game. As he rushed out he caromed against a very well-dressed,

Papa Bouchard

portly, clean-shaven elderly gentleman, who was parading into the garden
with a great air of pomposity. In his
hand he held conspicuously a newspaper, on the first page of which was a
large photogravure easily recognizable as
himself, and under it, in letters an inch
long, were the words,

DR. DELCASSE

THE MOST CELEBRATED ALIENIST
IN PARIS.

Below this was the cut of a handsome
building, and under this was inscribed,
" The Private Sanatorium at Melun of
Dr. Delcasse."

Dr. Delcasse seemed to feel the in-
jury to his dignity very much when
de Meneval jostled by him so unceremoniously, nearly knocking him down.
He stopped, scowled, growled, and then,
with a portentous air of being much
displeased, stalked forward, took a seat
close to where Madame Vernet was
standing, and began pompously to unfold

his newspaper, always keeping the picture to his audience, so to speak —

which audience consisted solely of Madame Vernet.

Now, for quickness and boldness of resource Madame Vernet was fully the equal of de Meneval or any man alive,

and the moment she became convinced
of the identity of Dr. Delcasse a plan
was formed in her mind. Everybody
knew Dr. Delcasse, and also of the
war waged between him and Dr.
Vignaud, another celebrated alienist,
which, if carried to extremes, would
have resulted in locking up half the
population of Paris as lunatics either
in Dr. Delcasse's sanatorium at Melun
or Dr. Vignaud's private hospital in
Paris.

Madame Vernet realized, in her
brilliant scheme, the value of time.
There was a train leaving for Paris in
ten minutes. If she could but make
the first train, getting away before
Monsieur Bouchard returned! She
determined to at least try for it. She
came near to Dr. Delcasse, and said,
in a silvery voice :

"May I ask if this is not the re-
nowned Dr. Delcasse — the man who
has restored the largest number of
persons, cured and sane, to their fam-

ilies, of any doctor for the insane in
the whole world ? "

To this insinuating address from a
remarkably pretty and attractive woman
Dr. Delcasse, as would any other man,
felt a warming of the heart, and he
replied, rising politely :

"You flatter me. I *am* Dr. Delcasse."

"Then," cried Madame Vernet,
taking out her handkerchief and pre-
paring to weep, "you are the man I
most desire to meet. Oh, how fortu-
nate it is for me that you are here! I
have a brother with me — a dear, good
young man, but whose mind has been
affected ever since a fall he had from
an apricot tree some years ago. For
a year I had him at Dr. Vignaud's
hospital for the insane — rightly named,
for I think anyone who went there
would shortly be insane. Dr. Vignaud is a charlatan of the worst
description." Dr. Delcasse smiled in
a superior manner to hear himself

praised and Dr. Vignaud reviled — how delicious! "I am my poor brother's guardian," continued Madame Vernet, producing her card, inscribed "Madame Vernet, *née* Brion." "My brother's name is Louis Brion. Ever since he was released from Dr. Vignaud's asylum he has been much crazier than when he went in, although Dr. Vignaud declared him thoroughly cured."

"Just like Vignaud!" remarked Dr. Delcasse, with that spirit of fraternity which sometimes distinguishes the medical profession.

"This evening," continued Madame Vernet, throwing her most pleading and fascinating look into her eyes, "I brought my poor, dear brother out to this place to supper, thinking it would divert him. But he has been quite insane in all his actions, and just now he became violent. He took it into his head that this necklace I wear —which I may say to you confidentially

is paste — is real, and is worth forty
thousand francs, and that I have
stolen it from his wife. The poor
boy has no wife. And while I was
trying to soothe him just now he suddenly broke away, nearly knocking
you down as you came in, and declared he was going after the police to
arrest me — *me*, his devoted sister!"
Madame Vernet's voice became lost
in her lace handkerchief.

"I saw an unmistakable gleam of
insanity in his eye as he rushed by
me," said Dr. Delcasse, promptly.
"My experience, Madame, has been
vast. I can tell an insane patient at
a glance, and I have no hesitation in
saying that the young man gave every
indication to a practiced eye of being,
as you say, very much unbalanced.
And Vignaud said he was cured! Ha,
ha!"

"But the great thing," said Madame
Vernet, with real and not pretended
anxiety, "is to get him away from

here without scandal, and into your sanatorium, where I wish to place him under your care. How can that be managed ? "

" Nothing easier, Madame," replied Dr. Delcasse, eager to get hold of one of Dr. Vignaud's patients. " I am well known here — indeed, I am personally acquainted with many of our police officers. When the young man returns with the officers I shall simply, with your permission, direct them to convey him to my sanatorium — it is less than half a mile from here — and I will telephone to my assistant to have a strait-jacket, a padded cell and a cold douche ready for the unfortunate young man, and we will take care of him, never fear. When I release him, depend upon it, he will be actually cured. I am not Dr. Vignaud, I beg you to believe."

At this moment de Meneval, with a couple of officers, was entering the garden. The police station, as he

had said, was but two minutes away.
Dr. Delcasse, accompanied by Madame
Vernet, coolly advanced, and recog-
nizing the officers, spoke to them civilly, saying:

"Good-evening, Lestocq; good-
evening, Caron." And then to de
Meneval he said, soothingly: "Good-
evening, Monsieur Brion. I am pleased
to see you and your charming sister at
Melun, and think you will enjoy your
stay with me."

De Meneval looked from one to the
other in amazement, and opened his
mouth to speak; but before he could
get out a word Madame Vernet laid
her hand on his arm and said, in the
tone of soothing a raving lunatic:

"Yes, dear Louis, Dr. Delcasse
will take the best possible care of you,
and I will come out to see you every
week."

De Meneval found his tongue then.

"To the devil with Dr. Delcasse!
I never heard of him before. Police,

arrest this woman. I can prove by my wife and by a gentleman now in this garden that the diamond necklace this person wears is the property of my wife."

"Do nothing of the kind," interrupted Dr. Delcasse, with quiet authority. "This young man, Louis Brion, is the brother of this lady, Madame Vernet. He is demented, and his latest hallucination is that Madame Vernet has stolen the necklace she wears; that it is worth forty thousand francs, that she stole it from his wife — and he has no wife."

"But I tell you," shouted de Meneval, quite beside himself, "that I never saw this woman before. She has my wife's diamond necklace, and I can prove it. Call Monsieur Bouchard!"

"You see how it is," coolly remarked Dr. Delcasse to the two police officers, "the only thing is to get him out of the way as quietly as possible. I shall take him at once out to my sanatorium, where

The police officers seized him, and dragged him out, under Dr. Delcasse's direction.

Papa Bouchard

I will have a strait-jacket, a padded cell and a cold douche waiting for him."

With this the Doctor suddenly whipped out his silk handkerchief, and with the greatest ingenuity bound it fast round de Meneval's mouth, so that he was completely gagged and silenced. The police officers seized him, and dragged him out, under Dr. Delcasse's direction. De Meneval fought like a tiger, but it was one to three. The struggle, though violent, was noiseless, and before the two or three waiters in the vicinity realized what was going on everything was over, and Madame Vernet, picking up her gloves, fan and other belongings, scurried off another way to make the ten o'clock train.

Meanwhile, the interview between Papa Bouchard and Léontine had been stormy. Léontine had demanded an explanation, but Papa Bouchard had no satisfactory one to give. At first he mounted his high horse, declared Léontine's suspicions intolerable, and refused to discuss the subject of the necklace at all. But she was not so easily put off.

"If you refuse me an explanation," she said at last, "I shall simply confess all to Victor, and you will have to treat with a man instead of a woman."

"Do; confess all to Victor," replied Papa Bouchard, tartly. "Tell him that sociological yarn you told me."

"I'm afraid to," replied Léontine, so dolefully, that it partially softened Monsieur Bouchard, who really had a good heart.

"Come, come, now," he said. "You had better take my word for it when I tell you that, in spite of appearances, your necklace is safe. I can't and won't tell you the circumstances — you and de Meneval would both blazon it over Paris, and it would be devilish uncomfortable — " Papa Bouchard was becoming expert in the use of bad language — "it would be devilish uncomfortable for me. I can straighten the

174

Papa Bouchard

whole thing out in a few days, if you will only keep quiet. *Can't* you keep quiet ? "

By this time they were re-entering the garden.

" I will agree to keep quiet for a week," said Léontine, firmly. " At the end of that time, if this unpleasant complication about my necklace is not cleared up, I have a presentiment that the whole thing will get into the newspapers. Just fancy the headlines, ' Mystery of Madame de Meneval's Diamond Necklace. Monsieur Paul Bouchard Proved to have Given it to an Adventuress, With Whom he was Caught at the Pigeon House.' "

Papa Bouchard felt his knees grow a little weak under him, and went and sat down in the chair he had lately vacated. Léontine followed him and said dramatically, as if reading the scare head in a great metropolitan daily.

" ' SUICIDE of Monsieur Paul Bouchard ! The late Advocate Discovered

175

Papa Bouchard

in his Apartment With a Pistol Wound Through his Temple! The Apartment presents the Appearance of a Shambles! Blood Over Everything!! Walls and Ceilings Much Bespattered!!!'"

Papa Bouchard, very white around the lips, poured out with an unsteady hand a glass of champagne, and drank it, the glass clinking against his teeth.

"Léontine," he said, after having drained the glass. "You are trying to frighten me. But you can't do it. You sha'n't do it. And I insist that you shall not be carrying any of your sensational tales to the Rue Clarisse, alarming my poor sister, and making her life a torment. Do you hear me?"

"Yes, indeed, I do," replied Léontine. "And, by the way, where is your lady friend?"

Monsieur Bouchard looked around for Madame Vernet, and was much disturbed at not seeing her. In the perplexities and annoyances of the last half-hour he had made up his mind that it was absolutely necessary to get that diabolical necklace back, and to work himself out of the scrape in which he unexpectedly found himself.

He called up François, who reported that Madame Vernet had gone out in a great hurry. There was a train for Paris just leaving. It struck him Madame was trying to make that train. Such was precisely Monsieur Bouchard's idea. Her departure in this way seriously annoyed and alarmed him. One thing, however, was clear in his mind — he must get back to Paris as soon as possible. There was another train in twenty minutes, and then there would be no more till eleven.

De Meneval's disappearance was also strange, but just as Léontine was beginning to feel uncomfortable she saw de Meneval approaching. Something unusual had evidently happened. He looked angry and excited, and his usually immaculate dress showed that he had been in a scrimmage. By his side walked the portly, the imposing Dr. Delcasse. The Doctor was apologizing to de Meneval with the utmost earnestness.

"My dear sir, I beg you will believe it was a most extraordinary mistake——"

"*Very* extraordinary!" replied de Meneval, grinding his teeth with rage.

"If I had succeeded in getting you into my sanatorium you would have found every comfort awaiting you."

"Yes, a strait-jacket, a cold douche, and a padded cell, as you kindly promised me."

"May I ask, Monsieur, that you will not spread this unfortunate story abroad in Paris?"

"I shall have it printed in every newspaper in Paris to-morrow morning, and I shall myself write to Dr. Vignaud, giving him a detailed account of the affair."

"Good heavens!"

"And if insanity ever develops in my family, it is Dr. Vignaud who shall

treat every case — every case, do you
hear ? ''

"Then, sir," said Dr. Delcasse, angrily, "all I have to say is that I am
not at all sure my first diagnosis was

not correct, and you are indeed, already
crazy — and I have the honor to bid
you good-evening."

"Go to the devil!"

Dr. Delcasse, slapping his hat down
angrily on his head, marched indig-

nantly out, and de Meneval, still furious
at the treatment to which he had been
subjected, poured out his injuries :

" And but for having been recognized by some of the waiters as I was
being dragged away I should at this
moment be an inmate of a lunatic
asylum, sent there by the wiles of a
shameless adventuress, brought to the
Pigeon House by Monsieur Bouchard."
This was de Meneval's exact language.

" Take care, sir ; take care ! " cried
Papa Bouchard, in a voice trembling
with wrath. He was not accustomed
to being talked to in that manner.
" You may repent of this language.
Madame Vernet is a lady of means and
respectability. I did not bring her out
here. She came expecting to find here
her uncle and aunt, who live in Melun.
I invited her to sup in a public place,
as any gentleman is authorized to do in
the case of a widow old enough to take
care of herself — and because your suspicions were excited by her having on

a necklace like that you bought for your wife, you proceeded to make trouble. Well, it seems she turned the tables on you very cleverly, and no doubt, being a bashful little thing, she dreaded the sensation it would make and the notoriety which might follow, and — and so, naturally, has gone." Then, turning to Léontine, Papa Bouchard played his trump card. " Have n't you your diamond necklace safe at home, Léontine ? "

" To which Léontine faltered : " Y—y—yes, Papa Bouchard."

" Well, then," cried Papa Bouchard, assuming an air of triumphant virtue to poor de Meneval, " I hope you see the enormity of your conduct."

" I can't say I do," sullenly replied de Meneval.

" Very well, very well," continued Papa Bouchard, realizing that he held all the trumps in the game. "Do you want to go into the whole business of this necklace ? If you do there is no time like the present. Do you, Léontine, want the matter sifted to the bottom ? "

De Meneval remained gloomily silent, while Léontine murmured, " N— no, Papa Bouchard."

Papa Bouchard, having thus effectually silenced both of them, felt master of the situation, but all the same, he was desperately anxious to reach Paris in advance of the de Menevals, so that he could get on Madame Vernet's track before they should. He was pretty sure that she could not slip away from her apartment without leaving some trace. There was another train going almost immediately, and there would be no more till eleven o'clock. It would be exceedingly convenient for him to get an hour's start of the de Menevals. So it occurred to him that if he were to propose a little more champagne Léontine and de Meneval would never run away and leave it, but *he* could and would.

Papa Bouchard

"Now," said he, with an air of benevolence, "everything having been straightened out about the necklace, suppose we have a bottle of champagne before returning to Paris. Here, waiter!"

François immediately responded with a bottle of champagne.

De Meneval had never supposed that anything would be too pressing to drag him away from good champagne, but he inwardly swore, as Léontine silently fretted, at the delay that might prevent him from making the next train to Paris. Both of them gulped down the champagne rather than drank it, while Papa Bouchard, alleging that he had already taken several glasses, declined any more. Every moment or two he looked at his watch, and he said to Leontine:

"Will you be going back to Paris to-night, Léontine?"

"Indeed I shall," eagerly replied Léontine. "I shall go back with you."

" But I sha'n't be going back till the midnight train. You see I am beginning to keep late hours, to make up for lost time, and that will be too late for you. Why can't you remain at de Meneval's quarters ? "

" I have an engagement early to-morrow morning," replied Léontine, who was determined to get to Paris as quickly as she could and make some private inquiries on her own account concerning Madame Vernet. The same intention was fixed in de Meneval's mind. Therefore he said :

" Never mind, Léontine ; I am off duty till twelve o'clock to-morrow, and I will take you to Paris to-night, if you wish."

At which Léontine, looking very blank, replied :

" Oh, very well. That will be nice."

" Now, why are you in such a hurry to get to Paris ? " asked Papa Bouchard. " The next train is always crowded —

not a seat to be had in a first-class
compartment for love or money, and
it makes a stop of only two minutes
and a half;
unless one is
already at the
station it is
almost impos-

sible to make it, and
you see it is now within
a few minutes of the train."

While Monsieur Bouchard was speak-
ing he was putting on his gloves and
making for the garden door, and the
de Menevals, each carefully avoiding

an appearance of haste, were following him. Everybody had forgotten that the champagne was not paid for, except François.

"So," kept on Papa Bouchard, still edging away, "you will go by the late train; perhaps I'll wait for it myself."

At that moment the shriek of the locomotive resounded. Immediately every pretense of waiting for the other train vanished. All three of them bolted for the exit to the garden. François rushed after them, bawling, "Your bill, Monsieur — the champagne — and the tip — " while the parrot, suddenly wakened from a nap, uttered a screech of demoniac laughter and began to yell after Papa Bouchard's rapidly retreating figure:

"Bad boy Bouchard! bad boy Bouchard!"

Chapter III

ANYONE who saw Monsieur Bouchard a week after his adventures at the Pigeon House would have said that the excellent man had grown ten years older in that time. For he had endured more cares, anxieties, worries, vexations, apprehensions and palpitations in that one week in the Rue Bassano than in all his thirty years in the Rue Clarisse. Not that Monsieur Bouchard had the slightest desire to go back to his old life. Not at all. In the Rue Bassano he at least lived; in the Rue Clarisse he had merely vegetated.

In the first place, on his arrival at his apartment shortly after midnight on that fateful evening spent at Melun he

Papa Bouchard

had been unable to find out anything at all about Madame Vernet. The *concierge* had gone to bed when he got home, and he dared not disturb the whole house at that hour. He spent a sleepless night, with Pierre snoring peacefully in the next room. The fellow had not come home till two o'clock in the morning. Monsieur Bouchard utilized the watches of the night in making up a story to tell the *concierge* to account for the enquiries he meant to make concerning Madame Vernet. A *concierge*, he well knew, is the nearest approach to an omniscient being on this planet. It was comparatively easy to concoct a tale that would go on four legs, in the expressive phrase of his countrymen. Monsieur Bouchard was vastly pleased with his own shrewdness when he paused to think of the facility with which he invented his story. But to get it accepted at its face value — ah, that was another thing.

At six o'clock in the morning he

tiptoed down stairs in his dressing gown and slippers. The *concierge*, yawning, was just opening the shutters in her little den.

" Can you tell me, my good woman," said Monsieur Bouchard, in a manner calculated to allay any suspicions the *concierge* might have — if anything can allay the suspicions of a *concierge* — " whether Madame Vernet arrived here last night — in fact, if she is in the house at present ? I ask because I promised her aunt and uncle out at Melun last evening to escort her in, and by some accident we became separated in the railway station, and I am considering what apology I shall make to her aunt and uncle — very worthy people at Melun."

The *concierge* looked at poor Monsieur Bouchard, not with suspicion, but with certainty in her eye. The very expression of her face called him a liar and a villain, as she replied, coolly :

" Madame Vernet *did* come in last

night and left the house at five o'clock this morning, to visit her aunt and uncle at Châlons."

By which Monsieur Bouchard, who was no fool, found out three things: first, that Madame Vernet had been beforehand with the *concierge*; second, that Madame Vernet did not have an aunt and uncle at Châlons, although she seemed to have uncles and aunts in every town, village and hamlet in France; and third, that wherever she might be she certainly was not at Châlons.

He spent the next three days in vain efforts to find out Madame Vernet's whereabouts. The *concierge* had evidently been thoroughly bought and coached, and would absolutely tell nothing. Madame Vernet had taken her apartment by the month, and had paid in advance. The *concierge* knew no more. Not even a ten-franc piece could screw any additional information out of her.

Papa Bouchard

Papa Bouchard began to feel a little frightened. What would happen if it should come out in the newspapers, as Léontine had threatened? There were journalists enough in Paris ready to jump at such a story as Léontine had hinted at. There was that Marsac, and the remarkable tale he had concocted about a bogus fortune — Papa Bouchard recalled at least a dozen instances that were frightfully like what he apprehended. When this thought occurred to him he bit the pillows in his anguish — it was in the middle of one of his sleepless nights. And what glee would those laughing devils of newspaper men have out of him! And how should he ever show his face in the Rue Clarisse? Monsieur Bouchard made up his mind that if ever the thing got into the newspapers he should emigrate to Madagascar.

Of course, Pierre knew all about it. Monsieur Bouchard had told him too much not to tell him more. Pierre

Papa Bouchard

was only moderately sympathetic, which infuriated Monsieur Bouchard.

"At least," cried the poor gentleman, "those two scamps, Léontine and de Meneval, are in as much trouble as I am."

"But they have the necklace," replied Pierre, "and it seems to me that Monsieur is in a jolly hole, with his necklaces and his widows, and all the rest of it."

Monsieur Bouchard, at this, burst into a string of bad words that were very reprehensible, but perfectly natural to a man in his imminent circumstances.

However Pierre might choose to devil his master in private, in public he was unflinchingly loyal to him. In the first place, Léontine and de Meneval, each determined to force an explanation from Monsieur Bouchard, haunted the Rue Bassano, and when they did not come they wrote. It was easy enough to dispose of the frantic notes

and letters, but when the two came —
always separately — and Léontine wept
and raved that she would and must see
Papa Bouchard, and de Meneval swore
and stormed to the same effect, Pierre
was immovable. Monsieur was one
day at Passy, another he was at Ver-
sailles, always on important business,
and Pierre never had the least idea
when he would be home. Thus, by
unceasing vigilance and an unabashed
front, Pierre managed to stave off an
interview between his master and the
de Menevals for the whole of a critical
week.

Mademoiselle Bouchard was easier
to manage. Pierre went to the Rue
Clarisse daily, with a very acceptable tale
about Monsieur Bouchard being so busy
making the will of a rich old gentleman at Passy that he had no time for
anything else; likewise, that he was
finding the noise and commotion of the
Rue Bassano so objectionable that he
bitterly regretted having left the Rue

Papa Bouchard

Clarisse. This little romance took so
well that Pierre improved on it by saying that Monsieur Bouchard was trying to sublet the apartment, so he could
return to peace and quiet in the Rue
Clarisse. Mademoiselle Bouchard was
touched, charmed, delighted to hear
this.

Not so Élise. She was not of a
trusting or confiding nature. When
Pierre turned up, late in the day,
yawning, and still only half-awake,
she did not believe in the least his
account of being kept awake by the
noises of the carts and carriages in
the Rue Bassano. She boldly taxed
him with leading a riotous life, which
Pierre strenuously denied, and going
to Mademoiselle Bouchard, actually
wept over Élise's want of confidence
in him after thirty years of married
life. Mademoiselle sharply rebuked
Élise, and ordered her henceforth to
believe everything Pierre told her.
Élise made no reply to this beyond

Papa Bouchard

her usual sniff, but privately resolved the first day she had time to slip around to the Rue Bassano and interview the *concierge*. She knew the ways of *concierges* as well as the ways of men.

For four days Monsieur Bouchard gave himself, body and bones, to the business of a private detective in trying to locate Madame Vernet. Vain effort! He of course expected to have to pay handsomely for the return of the paste necklace, but he valued his peace of mind more than money, and was ready enough to come down with some cash provided he could get hold of the necklace.

On the fifth day he was delighted, but scarcely surprised, to receive a letter from Madame Vernet saying that, as there seemed to be some complications concerning the necklace he had so generously and sweetly given her, and as she was a person of much delicacy of feeling, she was seriously thinking of returning it. He could address her at the Pigeon House at Melun.

Monsieur Bouchard replied by writing and flatly offering her five hundred francs, nearly six times the original value of the necklace. He himself took his letter out to the Pigeon House, and spent the entire evening there, on the chance that Madame Vernet might turn up. She did not, however. Next day he received a letter from her, all reproaches and hysterics ; how could he offer her money ! — her, the most disinterested, the most retiring of her sex ! Money was nothing to her, least of all a trifling sum of five hundred francs. Monsieur Bouchard promptly replied, increasing his offer to a thousand francs. Another deeply injured note from Madame Vernet. At last, after five days of continual negotiation, Monsieur Bouchard haunting the Pigeon House every evening, terms were arranged — two thousand francs in exchange for the necklace.

Papa Bouchard

It was infamous, but as Pierre reminded Monsieur Bouchard, one must
always pay for one's indiscretions.
It would seem as if Madame Vernet
had the direct inspiration of Satan
himself in dealing with the too amiable
and too susceptible Monsieur Bouchard.
Not only had she given her address
all along as the *Pigeon* House, but
she appointed that abode of gayety
and champagne as the rendezvous
where she was to meet Monsieur
Bouchard and hand over the necklace
in return for two thousand francs
in notes of the Bank of France—
Madame Vernet specified that there
should be no cheque in the affair; she
was so diffident; it always embarrassed
her to go to a bank, and notes could
be passed anywhere.

But Monsieur Bouchard was not
wholly without discretion. He concluded he would rather not be seen in
the act of handing over the money to
Madame Vernet. Pierre — the foxy

Papa Bouchard

Pierre — should give her the money and should receive the necklace. So, on the evening specified, the two took the train for Melun, and went rattling out of Paris without dreaming of what was brewing be-hind them and likewise stewing ahead of them.

It was simply this : Élise had that evening found her opportunity to go around to the Rue Bassano, and in five minutes she had discovered everything Monsieur Bouchard and Pierre had been doing since they left the Rue Clarisse. The *concierge* knew all about the chase after Madame Vernet, the continual trotting out to Melun — nay, she knew that both Pierre and his master had an appointment with Madame Vernet at

Papa Bouchard

the Pigeon House that very evening.
Élise returned, boiling with rage, to
the Rue Clarisse, and with face and
eyes blazing recounted to the trembling and agitated Mademoiselle Bouchard the horrid story of the frightful
goings on in the Rue Bassano. And
she had for audience not only poor
Mademoiselle Bouchard, but Léontine
de Meneval, who happened to be paying her weekly visit to Rue Clarisse.
Léontine scarcely heard Élise's fierce
denunciations of the two reprobates
in the Rue Bassano; all she really
took in was the correspondence and
the running to and fro about the necklace. She flew from the apartment,
leaving Mademoiselle Bouchard in a
state of collapse on the sofa, while
Élise retailed every circumstance of
horror she had found out about the
renegades. Calling the first cab,
Léontine drove rapidly home, rushed
to her strong-box, and got the supposed paste necklace out. She had

Papa Bouchard

said to Monsieur Bouchard that anybody could tell at a glance that it was

an imitation, yet it so glowed and
sparkled in its white radiance that for
the first time she began to suspect it

was real. If so, it only deepened the mystery, and she felt she must solve it then and there. Again ordering a cab, she sprang into it and ordered the cabman to drive her to one of the great jewelry shops in the Avenue de l'Opéra. On reaching it she ordered the carriage to wait, and going into the shop, asked to see the proprietor. He advanced, politely, and Léontine, taking the necklace from about her neck, where she wore it under her high bodice, said, with such calmness as she could muster:

"Will you kindly give me some idea of the value of this?"

The jeweller took it up, examined it for a moment, and said:

"About forty thousand francs, I should say, Madame. The stones are remarkably well matched, better than in many costlier necklaces."

"Do you mean to say the stones are — are ——"

"Well matched, Madame. In fact,

some of them came from this establishment. It was made by M. Leduc, a
friend of mine, and I assisted him."

"Thank you," replied Léontine,
forcing herself to be calm, reclasping
the necklace round her throat and covering it up. She went out, got into the
cab again, and hesitated before giving
her order. She was in truth quite
dazed and mystified. The man had
touched his hat three times, when she
said, with an air of quiet determination:

" To the St. Lazare station."

Yes, she would that very moment
go and confess all to Victor. Her resolution seemed an inspiration. There
was some mystery about the necklace,
and it was only fair that Victor should
know it. There should be no more
concealments between them. She
reached the station just in time to miss
the eight o'clock train. It was still
daylight, and she waited for the next —
a very slow one. Half-way to Melun
the engine broke down. It was nearly

Papa Bouchard

eleven o'clock before she found herself
in front of the huge old barrack building
in which de Meneval had his quarters.

The orderly who took the place of

concierge at once recognized her and
politely escorted her to Captain de
Meneval's door.

"I do not think Monsieur le Capitaine is in at present," he said; "but
if Madame will wait, he will no doubt

be here shortly." And he knocked loudly at the door.

It was opened by a soldier — de Meneval's servant — whom Léontine had never seen before. The man's unfamiliar face, and the unlooked-for sight that met her eyes as soon as she stepped over the threshold, made her turn as if to go out. In the middle of the room was spread a table, with preparations for an elaborate supper; and Léontine's quick eye discovered that ladies were expected, for to three huge bouquets were appended cards with names written on them. "For the Sprightly Aglaia," "For Olga, the Queen of the Dance;" "For Louise of the Fairy Foot."

Léontine, slightly embarrassed, said to the soldier:

"I see I have made a mistake. I am Madame de Meneval, and I supposed these to be Captain de Meneval's quarters, but evidently they are not!"

Papa Bouchard

"They are, Madame," replied the man, very civilly.

"But I say they are *not!*" replied Léontine, somewhat tartly. "Captain de Meneval *never* entertains ladies at supper. He leads a most retired life at Melun, while here are preparations made for a gay party."

"Pardon, Madame; but Monsieur le Capitaine is giving the party to some young ladies from the Pigeon House."

Léontine's first impulse was to box the soldier's ears, but in sweeping another glance round the room she recognized her own picture over the mantel, together with a battered photograph of de Meneval's chum, Major Fallière, and other things to convince her that Captain de Meneval was really the host of the impending supper party. She retained self-possession enough to say to the man:

"If you have finished you may go." And he discreetly vanished.

Léontine, throwing her parasol on the

sofa, began to march up and down the room in wrath and excitement.

" *These* are his quiet evenings! *He* does n't know anything about the Pigeon House since he was married! I should n't have minded it if he had told me all about it, but to pretend to such economies, and at the same time be secretly indulging in these extravagances — these shameless orgies — oh, it is too much! "

Léontine had completely forgotten Putzki and Louise and the object of her sudden descent on her husband. While she was walking up and down, becoming every moment more angry and wrought up, the door opened, and in walked Major Fallière. Léontine recognized him at once from his picture — a soldierly looking man, slightly bald, immaculately well dressed, and bearing in his air the reason for his sobriquet, the Pink of Military Propriety. But his eye was not unkind; on the contrary, he was distinctly in the class

of men designated by women as dear
old things; and as such Léontine felt
an instant confidence in him.

The correct Major was not so correct, however, that he hesitated to
march up to Léontine, and chucking
her playfully under the chin, remarked:

" The Pigeons are out early to-night.
Where are the rest of the Pouters?"

Léontine's face was a study. A
flash of rage from her bright eyes was
succeeded by a look of puzzled help-
lessness, and then a radiant smile of delight. This was really too good. He
— old P. M. P. — had mistaken her,
Léontine de Meneval, for one of the
young ladies from the Pigeon House!
Angry as she was, she could not for-
bear laughing, and she replied, with her
sauciest air:

" Oh, they 'll be here presently. I
came early because I had a premonition
that old P. M. P. would be here early,
too. Always on time — one of the
cardinal virtues of a soldier." And

Papa Bouchard

then Satan tempted her to tiptoe and actually chuck old P. M. P. under the chin !

The effect frightened her for a moment or two, because Major Fallière, perfectly astounded and highly offended, drew himself up stiffly and glared at her like an ogre. But she was so very pretty, her impertinence was accompanied with such a charming air of simplicity, that no man not an absolute ogre could withstand it. So, in spite of himself, old P. M. P.'s backbone relaxed, his eyes softened and he tugged at his mustache to disguise the smile that *would* persist in coming.

Léontine having once admitted Satan

into her heart, he speedily took complete possession of the premises, and the next thing he inspired her to do was to examine the prim Major carefully from the top of his thinly thatched head down to the tips of his well-fitting shoes, and say to him :

" I have often heard of you, and I am so glad to meet you. You know you are quite a handsome man, Major."

The Major grinned.

" For your age, that is."

The Major scowled.

" And I like you well enough to wish to make friends with you. But first I must tell you my name. It is Satanita."

" Satanita ! Rather suggestive, eh ? "

" I should say so. Little Satan ; and I match my name."

" You are the sweetest, most innocent and captivating little devil I ever saw."

" Thank you. You should see me dance and hear me sing. The Pouters, as you call them, are not a patch on me."

" I can well believe it."

" I have another name — I am called the Queen of the Harem-Scarem."

" No doubt you are."

" Now," continued Léontine, seating herself with a confidential air beside Major Fallière, "what do you think of our host, Victor de Meneval ? "

" One of the best fellows in the world."

" Devoted to his wife, eh ? "

" Yes. I have never seen her, but I hear she is a charming creature, and Victor is truly attached to her."

" This looks like it, does n't it ? " cried Léontine, pointing to the supper table.

" I don't see that it does n't look like it. I happen to know that de Meneval has had a good deal to trouble him lately. He got some money from an unexpected source some days ago, and

Papa Bouchard

I advised him to give a little supper —
it's dull out here, you know ———"

" *You* advised him to give a little
supper! You — the Pink of Military
Propriety!"

"Yes, why not?"

"And how about his wife?"

"Oh," replied the Major, with easy
confidence, "she would probably make
an awful row if she knew it — but
she'll never know it. De Meneval has
coached me — I know exactly what to
tell Léontine when I meet her — it so
happens that I have not met her yet.
But I hear she is a charming young
woman."

"She will be twice as charming to
you when she finds that you have been
leading her husband off into giving
suppers to — to — little devils like me
for example," said Léontine, very
solemnly.

"Oh, de Meneval and I have mapped
out our campaign. We have a large
and trusty assortment of lies, expressly

for Léontine's consumption, and she will swallow every one of them."

Now, this was very provoking of the Major, but something in his kind eyes, his way of standing up for Victor, his candid praise of herself, gave Léontine a sudden impulse to tell him the whole story of what was weighing on her and perplexing her and had driven her out to Melun at that hour of the night. She knew all about him, what a generous, sympathetic fellow he was, in spite of his primness and propriety — in short, that he was a dear old thing. So, with eyes flashing with mischief, and with smiles dimpling her fair face, Léontine said, demurely :

"I have still another name besides Satanita and Queen of the Harem-Scarem. Can't you guess it?"

"No. I am not a clairvoyant."

"I am — " Léontine rose, with her whole face sparkling with impish delight — "I am Léontine, Madame de Meneval, wife of your friend, Victor de

Meneval. Yonder is my picture. Here am I."

Poor P. M. P! He stared at her for a full minute, glared wildly about him, and then, jumping up, made a dash for the door, from which Léontine, laughing till the tears ran down her cheeks, dragged him back.

" What are you running away for ? " she asked, forcing him to a seat beside her.

" Because — because — " the Major tore his hair, " oh, de Meneval will certainly shoot me when he hears that I chucked you under the chin ! "

" But he won't hear it, unless you tell him. And *I* chucked *you* under the chin, remember."

Major Fallière, burying his head in his hands, groaned aloud, and then all at once the absurdity of the thing struck him, and he burst into a howl of laughter.

Léontine joined him. They laughed and laughed, and when they would

get a little quiet Léontine would motion as if to chuck him under the chin
again, and Fallière would go off into
renewed spasms.

Presently, however, Léontine grew

grave. The instant success of her im-
promptu personation had given her an
idea. She wanted revenge — a sharp
revenge — on de Meneval, and she saw
a way to get it.

"Listen, and be quiet," she said to

Papa Bouchard

Fallière. "Victor deserves to be punished. I will tell you why. He has always represented to me that he led the quietest kind of a life here — nothing but attention to his military duties, and his evenings spent in the seclusion of his own room, with nothing but ballistics and my picture for company."

Fallière could not refrain from a soft whistle.

"And he professed to be so glad that you were ordered to Melun, because you were so much more sedate than the other officers. He complained that they spend too much time at the Pigeon House, while he had entirely given up frequenting that fascinating place."

Fallière whistled a little louder.

"I had the greatest difficulty in persuading him to take me to supper there the other night. Now, what do I find? That he has been throwing sand into my eyes all the time.

Look!" Léontine waved her arms dramatically toward the table. "Ought n't he to be punished?"

"Certainly he ought," replied Fallière, with the ready acquiescence of a bachelor who thinks that married men should be made to toe the line.

"Very well. You will help me?"

"You may count on me."

Léontine rose and looked around her. On the sideboard sat a couple of bottles of mineral water, and on the floor near by a wine cooler full of bottles of champagne. She cleverly transferred the labels from two of the champagne bottles to the apollinaris bottles and then put them in the wine cooler.

"I think I can drink at least a quart of apollinaris," she said.

"And I'll see that you get apollinaris every time," replied that crafty villain of a Fallière, laughing.

"And I'm Satanita, and I shall act Satanita until I have made Victor

Papa Bouchard

sorry enough he ever played me any
tricks."

"Oh, no, you won't! At the first
sign of distress on his part you will
throw the whole business to the winds,
fall on his neck and implore his for-
giveness. I know women well."

"Of course you do — having never
been married. But wait and see if I
don't give him a bad quarter of an
hour. And I reckon on your assist-
ance."

"I will stand by you to the last."

They were interrupted at this point
by a great sound of scuffling outside
the door, mingled with shrieks of girl-
ish laughter. The door flew open,
revealing three remarkably pretty
girls — Aglaia, Olga and Louise —
dragging in an elderly gentleman by
main force and his coat tails. The
elderly gentleman was resisting mildly
but with no great vigor, and it was
plain he was not particularly averse
to the roguish company in which he

217

Papa Bouchard

found himself. And the elderly gentleman was — Papa Bouchard!

One of these merry imps from the Pigeon House had possessed herself of his hat, which she had stuck on her

curly head; another one had laid violent hands on his umbrella, while the third and sauciest of the lot, Aglaia, had robbed him of his spectacles, which she wore on her tiptilted nose. Papa Bouchard, puffing, protesting,

Papa Bouchard

frightened, but laughing in spite of himself, was saying:

"Young ladies, young ladies, I really cannot remain, as you insist, to supper. I do not even know the name of the host on this occasion. I am quite unused to these orgies. I am out here this evening with my servant merely for the purpose of completing a business transaction."

A chorus of "Ohs!" and "Ahs!" saluted this speech, and Mademoiselle Aglaia, Papa Bouchard's chief tormentor, asked, solemnly:

"Is your business engagement with a lady or a gentleman?"

And when Papa Bouchard, in the innocence of his soul, replied, "It is with a lady," each one of the Pouters, as the young ladies of the Pigeon House were called, pretended to fall over in a dead faint.

Papa Bouchard, much alarmed, ran from one to the other, trying to revive them; but while he was rubbing

the brow and slapping the hands of
each in turn, Louise suddenly came to
life, and running and locking the door,
put the key into her pocket, so that
Papa Bouchard had no means of escape

except out of the third-story window
or up the chimney.

And at that moment his eye fell on
Léontine.

Pity Papa Bouchard! He really
had no intention of attending so gay
a party. He had spent the whole evening anxiously watching for Madame

Papa Bouchard

Vernet. She had not arrived, or at least had not seen fit to reveal herself, and while he was hovering about the entrance to the terrace garden looking for her, these three merry girls had come along, had swooped down on him without the least warning, and had carried him off bodily to de Meneval's supper. Papa Bouchard had not the slightest idea of where he was when he was plumped down in Captain de Meneval's room. But one look around him — the sight of Léontine — revealed his whole dreadful predicament to him. It was too much for poor Papa Bouchard!

His persecutors having permitted him to sit on a chair, he endeavored to recover himself, and fanning with his handkerchief in great agitation, he debated with himself what to do. Léontine, meanwhile, was laughing at him without a sign of recognition.

Papa Bouchard, presently finding his voice, said sternly to Léontine:

Papa Bouchard

"May I ask what you are doing here in this company?"

To which Léontine, with pert gayety, replied:

"And may I ask what *you* are doing here in this company?"

"I," said Papa Bouchard, with dignity, "am here by accident, and by the violence of these young women."

"Oh, what a fib!" cried Olga. "The old duffer begged us to let him come. We tried to shake him off, but we couldn't. Isn't that so, Aglaia and Louise?"

And Aglaia and Louise said it was so.

Papa Bouchard, astounded at such duplicity, glared at them, but the only satisfaction he got was a fillip on the nose from Aglaia and a remark to the effect that he and the truth didn't live at the same address. Papa Bouchard indignantly turned his back on these traducers and again opened on Léontine.

"I am amazed — amazed at your

temerity. What shall I say to Captain de Meneval when I see him, as I
shall to-morrow morning ? "

" Anything you like," was Léontine's laughing answer.

" Léontine de Meneval," cried Papa
Bouchard, much enraged, "do you
know *me*, your guardian and trustee ? "

" No, I don't," responded Léontine,
nonchalantly. " I never saw you before."

At this, shouts of laughter came
from the three young ladies, and they
all urged Papa Bouchard to stop his
wild career of prevarication and learn
to tell the truth.

Papa Bouchard, quite beside himself,
turned to Major Fallière.

" Sir," he said, solemnly, " you wear
the uniform of an officer, and I presume you are a gentleman. Believe
me, this lady — " indicating Léontine
— " is the wife of a brother officer of
yours, Captain de Meneval. The
truest kindness you can do him or her

is to persuade her to leave this scene of dissipation and return to Paris with me."

" O-o-o-o-h ! " shrieked the three

impish girls in chorus. " What an outrageous proposition ! And she says she never saw the man before ! "

Papa Bouchard, still appealing to Major Fallière, continued, earnestly :

" Perhaps this misguided girl has not

told you that she is Madame Victor de
Meneval."

" She told me," quietly replied Major
Fallière, "that she was simply Satanita,
a singer and dancer."

Papa Bouchard dropped limply on
the sofa and groaned in anguish of
heart. But now was heard a jaunty
step on the stair, which all recognized
as de Meneval's. The mischievous
Aglaia ran forward and unlocked the
door, and in stepped de Meneval,
smiling and debonair.

Now, this little festivity had been
his sole recreation during the ten miserable days since he had got into the
complication of the necklace; and the
supper, which was for only five, was at
the suggestion of the Pink of Military
Propriety. So it was without any com-
punctions that de Meneval walked into
his quarters, expecting to find a small
but jolly party. But he instantly
recognized the two uninvited members, and stopping short on the carpet,

his ruddy complexion turned a sickly green.

Papa Bouchard felt a sensation of triumph at Captain de Meneval's entrance. *He*, at least, would not dare to

deride and defy him, as these wretched young women had done. But before Monsieur Bouchard could open his mouth, Aglaia burst forth, pointing to the old gentleman :

" Of all the impudent men I ever saw, this one excels ! What do you think ? As soon as he found we were coming here to supper, he hung on to us — declared there was nothing he liked so well as a gay little party, that he could drink so much champagne he was called the Champagne Tank — and actually forced himself in here, although we tried to push him out. Did n't he, Olga and Louise ? "

And Olga and Louise confirmed every word that Aglaia uttered.

Papa Bouchard, thoroughly exasperated, struck an attitude like that of Socrates in his favorite picture, " Socrates and His Pupils," and addressed Captain de Meneval.

" Monsieur le Capitaine," he said, " you of course do not and cannot believe a word that these young ladies say concerning my presence here tonight."

Victor, very much alarmed, and dreading to catch Léontine's eye, yet retained enough of his wits to see that he had Papa Bouchard at a disadvantage, and that the best thing to do was to assume the worst, and decline to listen to any explanation.

"Monsieur Bouchard," he said, coldly, "you are asking a little too much of me when you wish me to believe your testimony against that of three ladies. I don't know how you came, but I am very glad to see you now that you are here, and hope you will remain to supper."

"But I came on business!" cried poor Papa Bouchard. "I had an appointment to finish up a transaction with a lady —— "

And Aglaia and Louise and Olga again uttered a chorus of shrieks, and pretended to faint.

But de Meneval had troubles of his own to attend to then. He walked over to where Léontine sat, and assuming an air of forced jollity, such as a man puts on when he anticipates a wigging from the wife of his bosom, said :

228

Papa Bouchard

"Delighted you happened to arrive, my love — and what do you think of the Pouters?"

"I think they are very jolly girls," promptly replied Léontine; "but as I am another uninvited guest, I thought it best to tell Major Fallière and the others that I, too, am a singer and dancer — Satanita, I called myself, on the spur of the moment."

De Meneval turned from green to blue. "And you did not immediately inform them that you are my wife?" he hissed, in a savage whisper.

"No," coolly replied Léontine, "and when Papa Bouchard recognized me, I declared I had never seen him before. I am little Satanita — good name, isn't it? — for this evening."

De Meneval, enraged and disconcerted beyond words, felt helpless. Suppose he were to proclaim the truth? Léontine, as if answering the thought in his mind, whispered, with cruel glee:

229

Papa Bouchard

"And if you say I am your wife I
shall simply deny it. Satanita I am
and Satanita I shall be, and I shall
live up to the part — of that you may
be sure."

De Meneval was in doubt whether
to laugh or to shoot himself. And

then there was a move
toward the table. The
girls were dragging Papa
Bouchard forward, who,
still very angry, was yet
not insensible to their
pretty and mischievous
wiles. Léontine, run-
ning up to Major Fal-
lière, demanded that he
sit next her at table, while de Meneval
found himself sitting opposite Léontine, and with indescribable feelings
saw her drink champagne, as he supposed, by the tumblerful. Fallière had
cleverly got hold of the two bottles of
apollinaris, and filled Léontine's glass
with the greatest assiduity.

Papa Bouchard

There was much noise and excitement, and as the supper progressed de Meneval grew almost frantic over the spectacle his dear little Léontine was making of herself. For she not only managed to drink innumerable glasses of apollinaris, but she sang, she even danced. She paraded up and down the room, singing, in her sweet, saucy voice, verses made up at the moment.

"Oh, I am the Widow Clicquot, Clicquot,
    I live at the Château Margaux, Margaux,
    My coachman's name is Pommery Sec,
    My footman is Piper Heidsieck,
    Moët-et-Chandon are my span."

She paused for reflection and added:

"And when Moët and Chandon go lame,
    I drive Mumm and Roederer!"

Papa Bouchard

Here her invention gave out, and rubbing the top of de Meneval's head with one of the champagne bottles, she added, laughing:

"Houp-là!"

That "Houp-là" almost drove de Meneval to distraction, but a roar of applause, in which all joined except her husband and Papa Bouchard, encouraged Léontine to continue. After a few moments' reflection she began singing again:

"This is the way in Champagne Land!
  Oh, Champagne Land is dear to me,
But Champagne Land is queer to me.
  There, lobsters grow on trees,
  There is a mine of cheese;
    The oysters walk,
    The cocktails talk,
And the *pâté de foie gras* builds his nest
In the hedge where the anchovy paste grows
    best."

And she concluded with another "Houp-là!"

At this Papa Bouchard, who had

been as much horrified as de Meneval, leaned over and whispered in
agony to him :

" She has certainly lost her mind
and appears quite crazy ! "

This was too much for poor de
Meneval. He had spent an hour of
torture while Léontine, vastly to her
own amusement, to Major Fallière's,
and to that of the Pouters, had ex-
hibited all the saucy graces of a Satanita, and Queen of the Harem-Scarem,
but de Meneval could stand no more.
Therefore, rising from the table, he
cried, with tears in his eyes :

" My friends, I beg of you to leave
me. This lady who calls herself Satanita is my wife. I have never seen
her act in this manner before — I am
sure she never so acted before. It is
my duty as well as my privilege to
shield her, and I wish to say that if
any person, man or woman, ever men-
tions what her unfortunate conduct
to-night has been, a life will be for-

feited, for I swear to shoot any man who dares to breathe one word against her, and any woman who does it may reckon on my vengeance." And with big tears rolling down his cheeks, he held his arms out to his wife.

This was too much for Léontine. Just as Major Fallière had predicted, at the first sign of repentance on de Meneval's part she forgot all her resolutions to punish him, and falling into his arms, she exclaimed, in her own, natural voice:

"You dear, chivalrous angel, I have n't touched champagne — it is nothing but apollinaris water, and I am your own true, devoted Léontine!"

De Meneval was so overcome that he could do nothing but pat her head and cry:

234

Papa Bouchard

" Oh, what have you not made me suffer to-night ! "

" At least," replied Léontine, laughing and looking toward Major Fallière, " you have not spent your usual dull evening at Melun," and de Meneval had the grace to blush, while old P. M. P. laughed back at the roguish Léontine.

Papa Bouchard, too, had suffered agonies at Léontine's behavior — agonies, however, which the attentions he experienced at the hands of the young ladies partly ameliorated, for they had not stopped pinching and tickling him for a single moment.

" Really," he said, " I have been very much agitated and distressed — I never saw such doings in the Rue Clarisse. I was very seriously concerned at my ward's behavior — very seriously concerned. But now," continued Papa Bouchard, " everything seems to be straightened out to everybody's satisfaction, and finding ourselves accidentally

together, why not finish up our evening
with a jollity which — er — did not —
er — exist, so far as I am concerned, in
the beginning? So I say — houp-là!"

Alas! at that very moment the
door opened softly behind him and in
walked Madame Vernet! She was
prettier, more demure and gentle
than ever before. Her black costume,
though highly coquettish, had a nun-
like propriety about it. She advanced with downcast eyes, and said,
timidly:

"I knocked and thought I heard
someone say, 'Come in.' I do not
know on whose hospitality I am trespassing, but I saw Monsieur Bouchard
enter half an hour ago, and as I must
see him on a matter of business, I
venture to ask for a word with him
here."

Monsieur Bouchard, at the sight of
her, seemed about to collapse. Not so
Captain de Meneval. He rose at once
and said, with an ironical bow:

Papa Bouchard

"Madame Vernet, you are trespassing on the hospitality of Captain de Meneval, the gentleman you adopted as a brother about ten days ago and handed over as a dangerous lunatic to Dr. Delcasse — who had a strait-jacket, a cold douche and a padded cell ready for him."

At this Madame Vernet assumed an attitude more shrinking, more timid than before, and falling on Monsieur Bouchard's shoulder, cried:

"Dear Paul, protect me from this dreadful person!"

Monsieur Bouchard was not at that moment able to protect anybody. He looked the picture of abject despair as he clutched the arms of his chair. He could only say, feebly:

"Go away! go away!"

"Is that the way you speak to your own Adèle!" cried Madame Vernet, burying her head on Monsieur Bouchard's reluctant bosom and bursting into tears. "Oh, what a change within

237

one short week! Last week it was
nothing but 'Dearest Adèle, when
will you name the day?' And now
it is 'Go away! go away!'" Madame Vernet's voice was lost in sobs,
but she continued to rub her left ear
vigorously into Monsieur Bouchard's
shirt front.

"It is false!" wailed Monsieur Bouchard, trying to escape from Madame
Vernet's left ear.

"Do you pretend to deny," sobbed
that timid and trustful creature, "that
only a week ago you gave me this?"
She took from her pocket the paste
necklace, and at the sight of it a shock
like a galvanic battery ran down the
backbones of de Meneval and Léontine. "And that when I found it to
be paste you offered me two thousand
francs, in humble apology for the attempt to deceive me?"

"It is false!" again cried Monsieur
Bouchard, almost weeping.

"And that we were to meet here

238

to-night in order to make exchange?
Oh, dearest Paul, we have had lovers'
quarrels before, but nothing like this!"

Monsieur Bouchard was too much
overcome by Madame Vernet's affectionate attentions to do more than
groan and try to push her away. But
de Meneval, walking coolly up to her,
quietly and very unexpectedly took the
necklace out of her hand, saying:

"This is the property of my wife,
and as such I take possession of it,
and call on Monsieur Bouchard to
make an explanation."

At this Madame Vernet uttered a
despairing shriek, and throwing both
arms round Monsieur Bouchard's neck,
screamed:

"You must avenge this insult, Paul!
And you must at least give me the
two thousand francs!"

But Monsieur Bouchard was so perfectly delighted with the notion that de
Meneval had the necklace and Pierre
the two thousand francs, that his coun-

tenance changed as if by magic. He
struggled to his feet, and after vainly
to disengage himself from Madame
Vernet's encircling arms, much to the
amusement of the three young ladies
and Major Fallière, cried:

"I am perfectly overjoyed to make
an explanation — an explanation that
will cause you, Léontine, and you, de
Meneval, to forget all the unpleasant
events of this evening. This necklace
is paste — and the one Léontine has is
real. You may remember, de Meneval, you came to my apartment a week
ago last Monday evening, bringing
Léontine's real diamond necklace with
you. You told me that when you
bought it for her you also bought an
imitation one for seventy-five francs,
which you kept a secret from her."

De Meneval, during this speech,
had lost his dashing and determined
attitude.

"I believe I did something of the
kind," he said, meekly.

Papa Bouchard

"And that you had, still unknown to Léontine, put the paste one in place of the real one ; and you threatened, if I did not advance money to pay a large bill you owed at the Pigeon House for things like this —" Monsieur Bouchard indicated the supper table and the guests with one wave of his arm — "you would take the necklace to the pawnbroker."

De Meneval turned to Léontine, and knowing what was coming, said, with a sickly smile :

"Dearest, will you forgive me ? "

"Indeed I will ! " replied Léontine, who knew more of what was coming than did de Meneval.

"Scarcely were you gone," continued Monsieur Bouchard, assuming his oracular manner, which sat rather awkwardly on him, as Madame Vernet persisted in nestling on his shoulder, "when in comes Léontine with the paste necklace, and for the same purpose — money or the pawnbroker.

Papa Bouchard

It at once occurred to me that she could not be trusted with any necklace on which she thought money could be raised — her debts were to tailors and dressmakers — so I gave her back her own necklace — she has it now — and told her it was paste, and she said it looked it. Then, just as I had got rid of her, in comes *this* lady — " Papa Bouchard made a desperate effort to shake off Madame Vernet,

but that diffident person only held on to him the more affectionately — " picked up the necklace, clasped it round her neck, and walked off with it, and I have spent the most miserable week of my life trying to get it back. I had arranged to give her the two thousand francs, which Pierre, my man, has in his pocket at this moment, when, owing to this lady's indelicate persistence in following me here, and in rashly exposing the necklace, she lost it, and I keep my two thousand francs. If I could find that rascal Pierre I could prove all I say."

And as if in answer to his name, the door was burst open, and in rushed Pierre, pale and breathless.

" Monsieur," he cried to Papa Bouchard, " all is discovered, and we are in the greatest danger. My wife Élise found out everything from the *concierge* in the Rue Bassano this evening. She went back to Mademoiselle Bouchard, and, if you please, both of them took the train for Melun to capture us — and just as I was coming to warn you I ran into them at the foot of the stairs. They had asked for Captain de Meneval's quarters, in order to get him to help them search for us. They are on the stairs now ! "

Papa Bouchard

Léontine and de Meneval, meaning
to let Monsieur Bouchard bear alone
the brunt of Mademoiselle Bouchard's
wrath, immediately scuttled into seats
against the wall, which they occupied

with great dignity.   Major Fallière,
who had heard of Mademoiselle Bouchard, got as far away from the girls as
he could, and they — Aglaia, Olga and
Louise — with much discretion ranged
themselves primly on a sofa at the
farthest end of the room.   But this left

Papa Bouchard

Papa Bouchard standing in the middle, with Madame Vernet embracing him tenderly. He, too, would have liked to flee, but he was literally frozen with terror, and unable to move or speak. And then the door came open, and in walked, or rather marched, Mademoiselle Céleste Bouchard and Élise.

Never in all his fifty-four years of life had Monsieur Bouchard seen his sister in such a state as she was at that moment. Her eyes sparkled, and her small figure was erect and commanding. Her emotions had made both her and Élise altogether forget the primness and propriety of their costumes, for which mistress and maid had been noted. Mademoiselle Bouchard's correct, elderly bonnet seemed to have caught the same infection of demoralization as Monsieur Bouchard, Pierre and Pierrot, for it sat at a most improper and dissipated angle. Her mantle was awry, she had on one white

glove and one black one, and a fringe
of white petticoat showed the agitation
in which she had dressed.

Élise was in somewhat the same condition, and she clutched a flower pot and
a gold-headed stick which had belonged
to Bouchard *père*, under the impression
they were a travelling bag
and an umbrella.

The sight that met their
eyes was Monsieur Bou-
chard apparently submitting
with willingness to Madame
Vernet's endearments, while
the lady herself sobbed out
upon his breast:

" Oh, Paul, dearest, pro-
tect your own Adèle from
that dreadful old woman ! "

Now, this was too much for any woman to stand. Mademoiselle Bouchard,
panting and trembling with wrath and
horror, sank into a chair.

" Élise," she gasped, putting her hand
before her eyes, " put up your umbrella

between me and that disgraceful sight.
I cannot look upon it."

Élise, equally agitated, made futile

attempts to convert the stick into an
umbrella, and then cried out :

"Oh, this is only a stick ! Perhaps
I put the umbrella in the travelling bag."
But failing to find an umbrella in the
flower pot, she collapsed into a chair

next her mistress, crying out : " When you, Mademoiselle, have finished with Monsieur Bouchard I 'll dispose of Pierre. Oh, the rascal ! "

Pierre, like his master, was dumb before the accuser. Not so Madame Vernet. She continued to appeal to Monsieur Bouchard :

" Oh, darling Paul, I am *so* frightened ! Why don't you send her away ? "

" But I am not your ' darling Paul ' and never was ! "

Poor Monsieur Bouchard was simply a pitiable sight, and the de Menevals, the Major and three girls were heartless enough to go into convulsions of silent mirth at his predicament. They, too, had nothing to say in Mademoiselle Bouchard's indignant presence. But that lady was determined to be answered.

" Paul," she said, in the tone of an inquisitor, " stop those shocking demonstrations toward that person and explain your conduct to me."

Papa Bouchard

" My dear Céleste," replied Papa Bouchard, in a faint voice and almost weeping, " if you could induce this lady to stop *her* demonstrations I should be the happiest man on earth. And there's no explanation to give. I'm the helpless victim of a designing woman."

At which Madame Vernet screamed and said, trying to kiss him :

" But I will forgive you, my own Paul. I know you don't mean what you say."

And Élise added to Monsieur Bouchard's anguish, and to Mademoiselle Bouchard's horror by crying out, " Mademoiselle, he isn't trying to get rid of her. He is tickling her and pinching her — I see him myself! "

Monsieur Bouchard thought he should have died of horror at this awful and baseless charge.

Apparently Madame Vernet was master of the situation, but Major Fallière, the cool, the resolute Fallière, came to the rescue. Going up quietly

to Madame Vernet, he deliberately
raised her face so he could look her
squarely in the eye.

"Madame Vernet," he said, "you
seem to have lost sight of that little incident of representing my friend, Captain
de Meneval, as your brother and a dangerous lunatic, and the trick you played on
Dr. Delcasse. Now, I happen to know
that Dr. Delcasse is determined to punish
you, if he can find you, and unless you
immediately leave these quarters and
leave Melun I shall inform Dr. Delcasse of your whereabouts, and you will
have a visit from the police."

Madame Vernet, seeing she had met
her match, disengaged herself from Monsieur Bouchard, to that gentleman's great
joy. Assuming an attitude and air of
great innocence, she said :

"I don't really understand what you
mean, or even who you are. But being
naturally a very diffident and retiring
person, I cannot stand the least unfavor-
able criticism, and I shall certainly leave

Papa Bouchard

this censorious and unsympathetic company."

Major Fallière ceremoniously offered
her his arm, escorted her to the
door, and opened
it. Madame Ver-
net paused on the
threshold.

"I go," she said,
"to seek refuge
and protection with
my aunt and uncle
in Mézières."

And the Major
shut the door after
her.

Mademoiselle
Bouchard then rose
majestically and advanced to Monsieur
Bouchard.

"And *you*, Paul," she said, "will seek
refuge and protection in the house of
your sister in the Rue Clarisse, where
you spent thirty happy and peaceful
years. You will there resume the orderly

and quiet life interrupted by your unfortunate excursion into the Rue Bassano. You will return to early hours and wholesome meals. You will have boiled mutton and rice, with a small glass of claret, for your dinner, and ten o'clock will be your hour for retiring. An occasional visit to a picture gallery or a museum will supply you with amusements far more intellectual than the orgies you have been indulging in at the Pigeon House."

Monsieur Bouchard, the image of despair, looked round him. Captain de Meneval and Léontine were in fits of laughter. The three girls, huddled together on the sofa, were tittering; the grim Major was smiling broadly. Even a worm will turn, and so did Monsieur Bouchard.

"I am sorry, my dear Céleste," he said, in a voice he vainly endeavored to make cool and debonair, "but what you suggest is impossible. I have taken my apartment for a year. And I find that

Papa Bouchard

boiled mutton and rice for dinner do not suit my constitution. I — I — I — shall remain in the Rue Bassano."

A round of applause from Major Fallière, Léontine and Victor, in which the three young ladies joined, much to Monsieur Bouchard's annoyance, greeted this. Nevertheless, it stiffened his backbone.

"Do you mean to say that you do not intend to return to the Rue Clarisse?" asked Mademoiselle Bouchard, in much agitation.

"Y—yes," replied Monsieur Bouchard, trying to assume a swashbuckler air. "You see, I don't think the air of the Rue Clarisse agrees with me very well. I often had twinges of rheumatism there. Now, since I have been in the Rue Bassano, my joints feel about twenty-five years younger. In fact, I myself feel considerably younger — an increased vitality, so to speak. I am sorry to disoblige you, my dear Céleste, but

Papa Bouchard

for the sake of my health and other reasons I shall remain in my present quarters."

Mademoiselle Bouchard, defeated, was speechless. Not so Élise. Walking up to Pierre, she seized him and bawled :

"No excuses about your health shall keep *you* from the Rue Clarisse. I promise you that you shall have a very different time there from your life in the Rue Bassano, turning night into day, running out here to the Pigeon House all the time and making a show and a scandal of yourself."

"No, Élise," firmly replied Pierre, who had much more real courage than his master, "I promised Mademoiselle Bouchard that I never would desert Monsieur Bouchard. If he remains in the midst of the dangers of the Rue Bassano he needs my protecting services more than ever. Although but a servant, I have a sense of honor. I cannot break my word."

254

Papa Bouchard

"Oh, you old hypocrite —" began Élise.

"Hypocrite, you may call me," answered Pierre, folding his arms and turning up the whites of his eyes, "but liar and falsifier you cannot. Mademoiselle —" to Mademoiselle Bouchard — "I shall keep my word to you. As long as Monsieur Bouchard remains in the Rue Bassano I stay with him. He shall not face alone the dangers  of that gay locale — those music halls, those theatres, those merry cafés, where all sorts of delicious, indigestible things are sold. His faithful Pierre shall be with him."

Mademoiselle Bouchard realized she was beaten. So did Élise. They

rose slowly. De Meneval ran into
the next room, and bringing out a
cage that held the redoubtable Pierrot,
put it into Mademoiselle Bouchard's
hand.

"There, dear Aunt Céleste," he
cried, "is your consoler. I offered
to buy him from the proprietor of the
Pigeon House, but the man said he
would give me the bird for nothing —
in fact, he would pay to get rid of
him. He was driving the customers
of the Pigeon House away by his
language."

"At least," said Mademoiselle
Bouchard, solemnly, "if men are
renegades, there is something of the
same sex that is faithful and grateful.
No doubt this poor bird is happy at
escaping from the dissipated atmosphere of the Pigeon House to the
sweet seclusion of the Rue Clarisse."

But, horror of horrors! The instant the wicked Pierrot found himself going in the direction of the

Papa Bouchard

door, on his way to the Rue Clarisse,
he broke out into the most outrageous
denunciations of the two ladies.
Shrieks, demoniac laughter, yells,

oaths and slang of the worst description poured from him; he screamed
with rage, bit furiously at both Mademoiselle Bouchard and Élise, and
forcing the cage door open, with almost human intelligence flew out and

perched on Monsieur Bouchard's shoulder, from which he continued his volley of abuse, winding up with a shout of:

" Go to the devil, you bowlegged old rapscallions ! "

But the two respectable elderly persons so infamously described, were already fleeing. Of course, no such bird as Pierrot had become could be tolerated in the Rue Clarisse, and Élise cried, while she and Mademoiselle Bouchard ran down the stairs:

" The only safe thing to do, Mademoiselle, is to keep everything masculine out of our apartment. They are all alike — men and parrots — everything that is masculine is abominable and not to be trusted. They live to deceive us poor women, and are never so happy as when they are lying to us. So let them go — Monsieur, Pierre and Pierrot — the wretches, and trust to retributive justice to overtake them ! "

But neither Monsieur Bouchard nor

Papa Bouchard

Pierre seemed to fear the blindfolded lady with the sword. They were at that moment capering with glee, and Pierre was shouting:

"I would n't go back to the Rue Clarisse for a million of monkeys!"

And Papa Bouchard was saying:

"I have a confession to make. It is this — that I like a gay life, and as that worthy fellow says, I would not go back to the Rue Clarisse for a million of monkeys, and all the money in the Bank of France beside. I intend to lead a *very* gay life, hereafter. I am a changed, a reformed man. Léontine, I shall allow you three-fourths of your income to spend — and if you get into straits, come to Papa Bouchard and perhaps I'll do something handsome. Victor, when next you have a little party of Pouters on hand, don't forgot your Papa Bouchard."

"Indeed I won't," cried de Meneval, "and Fallière and I will promise

Papa Bouchard

to get twenty of the best fellows in the
regiment and take you on the biggest
lark, bat, jag, and jamboree you ever
heard of in all your life !''

" Pray don't forget," answered Papa

Bouchard, while his mouth came open
as if it were on hinges. " Remember —
it is to have all the combined features
of a lark, a bat, a jag and a jamboree.
And Pierre, my man, we won't go
back to the Rue Clarisse ! ''

Papa Bouchard

" No ! " shrieked Pierre, capering in an ecstasy of delight, " we won't go back to the Rue Clarisse ! "

And Pierrot yelled as if inspired, " We won't go back to the Rue Clarisse ! We 're free ! we 're free ! Gay dogs are we ! "